Murder in Mind

A Mikdadi Mystery

By Catherine Mikdadi-Pattinson

Murder in Mind
By Catherine Mikdadi-Pattinson

First Published in 2015

Printed and Distributed through www.lulu.com

Cover design and Author photograph by Ray Pattinson

All rights reserved

Copyright Catherine Mikdadi-Pattinson

ISBN: 978-1-326-42433-6

Catherine Mikdadi-Pattinson has asserted her right under the Copyright, Designs and Patents Act, 1988 to be identified as the author of this work.

All the characters in this book are fictitious, and any resemblance to actual persons, living or dead, is entirely coincidental.

Dedication

To my family, without whom this book would not exist.
I hope they are as proud of me as I am of them.

To Agatha Christie, the undisputed authority on the village mystery.
I can only hope she would have enjoyed reading this book as much as I have enjoyed reading hers!

Contents

Introducing Constable Johnson	1
Enter Inspector Harbury	3
Sarah Talks to Inspector Harbury	9
The Chuckling Professor	13
Gemma Haines Has Her Say	20
Murder Is Not Childish	24
Mrs Quentin Has A Headache	35
Inspector Harbury's Tea	41
The Constable Meets His Match	47
Mayhew and Pickering	56
Afternoon Tea at the Hall	66
Inspector Harbury Acts	70
Constable Johnson's Breakfast	75
It is Only Polite to Knock	78
What Kind of Man Was Eddie	82
Amanda And Teddy	90
Inspector Harbury Takes Stock	93
A Visit To The Vicarage	95

Inspector Harbury Has Visitors	99
Marie Feels Better	107
Sarah Discovers a Secret	108
Sarah Has Another Shock	122
Harbury Gathers His Thoughts	133
Quiet Old Hisbury	137
Patrick In Two Places At Once?	140
Sarah Does Some Sleuthing	145
Exit Gemma Haines	164
Harbury Has a Little Idea	169
Plans Are Made	182
A Trip to Town	188
Brian Meets the Judge	197
A Call from Inspector Harbury	201
Harbury Makes an Arrest	204
The Judge Explains	213
Love Is in the Air	216
Brian Makes A Decision	220
The Judge Pays a Visit	222

Patrick Cooks Lunch and More	225
Inspector Harbury Asks Why	237
All Becomes Clear	239

Chapter 1

Introducing Constable Johnson

Constable Johnson remembered the feeling of dread he had experienced when Mrs Johnson had suggested moving out of London to be nearer her family. The thought of working as a police officer in a small village like Hisbury had terrified him but, having been in Hisbury for six months now, he was surprised to find how much he enjoyed village life. Granted, the vicarage cat did have a habit of climbing trees and getting stuck but the Reverand's sister, Mrs Woodgrove, did make the most delicious chocolate cake and there always seemed to be some spare for Constable Johnson when he dropped by.

Sighing contentedly, it occurred to the Constable that there was nothing like an English summer's evening. He couldn't have been happier as he continued his last walk around the village before heading home to Mrs Johnson's much praised steak and ale pie. He strolled past the school and the small village church and stopped in front of the wrought iron gates of the Hall. Hisbury Hall was the main house in the village and the home of Dr Eddie Saunders.

As Constable Johnson stood looking up at the imposing building, the warm evening air was suddenly pierced by a scream and a crash. The Constable stood paralysed for a moment and then rushed towards the front door. The door was opened by Dr Saunders, which in itself was unusual. A group of people stood in the hallway and as Constable Johnson entered the house, they turned their frightened faces towards him.

As the group moved back to let Constable Johnson through, he saw there was a body lying on the hallway floor with a young man kneeling beside it. The young man was Patrick Foley who lived locally. "It's Jeremy. He's dead," said Patrick, standing up. All eyes were on the Constable as he walked towards the telephone and lifted the receiver. "Operator, get me Inspector Harbury…..Inspector? Constable Johnson here, Sir. I'm at the Hall. I think you had better come over." The Constable paused to listen to the Inspector's reply and then replaced the receiver as he sadly saw the vision of his much-loved steak and ale pie disappear into the distance.

Chapter 2

Enter Inspector Harbury

Inspector Harbury was middle-aged, short and stocky with a clean-shaven face and a cheerful demeanour. He had been stationed in Hisbury since his days as a new Constable and so was well known locally.

He was shown into the living room by a nervous looking Marie, Dr Saunders' housemaid.

"Good evening, Sir." The Inspector addressed Dr Saunders as he appraised the assembled guests. "This is a nasty business."

"Indeed, Inspector. It has been a great shock to us. I appreciate you coming so quickly. We haven't moved anything so if you would like to look at the scene?"

"Thank you, Sir and then I will need to speak to your guests individually."

"Of course."

The Inspector turned to Constable Johnson who opened the living room door and stood back to let him through, closely followed by Dr Saunders.

The efficient figure of Johnson shut the door behind them.

Dr Saunders took Inspector Harbury and Constable Johnston into the hall where the body of the unfortunate Jeremy Marchington was lying with the police pathologist bending over him and then went back into the living room to join his guests.

"Evening, Tommy. What have we got here?" Inspector Harbury addressed the police pathologist whom he knew well.

"Evening, Harry. Well, there's no outward sign of injury but I'm sure things will be clearer once I've made a proper examination. I'll keep you posted."

"Thanks." And with this the Inspector asked Marie, who had been hovering in the background, to show him into the library and then go and ask Dr Saunders to come and see him. Marie led the Inspector across the hall and once he and Constable Johnson were comfortably installed in the library she hurried off to get Dr Saunders.

* * * * * * * * * * * * * * * *

"I can't believe it", Sarah's voice faltered a little and her hand went out and rested on Patrick's arm. He put his arm round her.

"Well dear, he was always rushing around, backwards and forwards to London and quite a socialite. It was bound to catch up with him," Mrs Quentin shrugged as if she was talking about something quite ordinary.

"How can you say that Mother? Besides, the police are here. They obviously don't think it was a natural death."

"Oh don't be absurd Darling, you're not seriously suggesting that one of us was involved. We didn't even see him." Mrs Quentin's voice had become quite high pitched and she had gone rather white.

"There, there, dear," Professor Quentin patted his wife on the arm and then addressed Dr Saunders. "We've all had a nasty shock. Perhaps we should ring for Marie, Eddie, and she could bring us some tea while we wait for the Inspector."

"Of course." Dr Saunders rang the bell and Marie appeared. She had red eyes from the shock of her discovery and her face betrayed the fear of her impending interview with the Inspector but also, he thought, a tinge of excitement at the novelty of the afternoon's occurrences.

"Marie, could you bring us some tea. I think we all need something to calm ourselves down and make sure that you have one too. You've had a nasty shock."

"Yes Sir," said Marie and then added. "The Inspector asked to see you in the library, Sir."

"Thank you, Marie. I'll go now." Dr Saunders followed Marie out of the room and went towards the library.

To Marie's disappointment everyone sat there quietly while Dr Saunders asked for the tea and although as she closed the door she could hear the low hum of voices, she could not make out what they were saying.

* * * * * * * * * * * * * * * *

Dr Saunders sat opposite the Inspector at the large oak library table in the centre of the room. Constable Johnson stood inconspicuously in front of the closed door holding his pad and occasionally noting something down in the unemotional way that he had as if he were writing a list of groceries. Dr Saunders felt suddenly very tired.

The Inspector watched him closely.

"If you could just take me through the day, Sir."

"Of course, Inspector. Well it started off much the same as any other day. You know I am a man of habit, Inspector. I have lived on my own since Marianne passed away and I am free to do things my own way. I usually get up at about 8 o'clock, I get dressed and come down for breakfast. After breakfast, I have coffee on the terrace if it's nice or in the sitting room just inside if not. After my coffee, I take a walk and then it depends on the whether I have any engagements or not. "

"And today?"

"Well, I spent the morning much as usual and then of course, we had to prepare for this evening's party. Sarah came over after lunch and we made sure everything was ready. Then she headed back home and I went into the village to run some errands. I had said I'd get someone in from the village to help with things for the party but Sarah enjoys organising these things. I think she has found it a little quiet here since she came back and of course there's that imagination of hers. I only really had the party for her. I mean she was so desperate for something to do. I felt if she didn't keep busy she would begin to imagine that something sinister was going on in the village just to relieve the monotony." Dr Saunders laughed and then checked himself.

"That's very interesting," the Inspector had risen and stood in front of the large open fireplace, one elbow leaning on the mantelpiece.

"I'm not suggesting that anything was wrong Inspector but this place is so quiet. I thought Sarah would need something to do to settle back into the village."

"So you don't think anything was wrong in the village? You hadn't noticed anything unusual?"

"Of course not." Dr Saunders shook his head. "I mean there must be a reasonable explanation for this. I've known Sarah and all these people for years and if there was something to know, I would know it." He paused and then continued. "As for Jeremy, he lived his life at full speed, he travelled a lot, I mean he could afford it and he's probably broken a few hearts but he was basically a good chap. I can't think of anyone who would want to harm him. I don't understand how this could have happened. He was just there in the Hall. We hadn't even seen him. We were all on the terrace. It must have been a heart attack or a seizure of some kind. He was only in his forties but these things do happen."

"That, Sir, is what we will have to find out. I wonder if you could ask Miss Quentin to step into the library."

"Of course."

Chapter 3

Sarah Talks to Inspector Harbury

Sarah walked across the Hall and approached the study door. She took a deep breath and knocked firmly on the door. It was opened by Constable Johnson.

"You wanted to see me, Inspector?"

"Yes, Miss Quentin. Please sit down and do not be alarmed. This is all routine. I just want to get a picture of what happened. Could you take me through your movements today?"

"Well, I came up to the Hall after lunch to help Uncle Eddie, I mean Dr Saunders, get ready for this evening. It was so lovely of him to have a welcome home party for me. I must admit that it's been a big change coming back to the village and I suppose he wanted me to feel more settled. Anyway, it gave me something to fill my time with. I arranged the flowers for the table centrepiece and I helped Cookie with the food. I was looking forward to it. People started arriving at about 7pm. My mother and father came first with Gemma, of course, then the Rev and his sister. Patrick arrived soon afterwards with his Uncle, Judge Seagrave, and finally Amanda and the faithful Teddy drove down from London. We all went onto the terrace for drinks. Amanda and Teddy were the last to arrive, well, except poor Jeremy. Uncle Eddie and I were just discussing whether we should get everyone into dinner or wait for Jeremy - he's always late - when there was a terrific crash and a scream. We all rushed into the hall and there he was, just lying there."

"Who reached Mr Marchington first, Miss?"

"Well, I think Patrick was there first but I was right behind him with Uncle Eddie and everyone else followed us out into the Hall."

"How did Mr Foley seem to you Miss?"

"Well, I mean we were all shocked, of course. You're not suggesting that Patrick was involved? He only reached the hall seconds before we did and Marie was there the whole time." Sarah's voice shook as she struggled to keep her composure.

"There's no need to get upset, Miss. We are just trying to get an idea of this evening's events. Sometimes people notice things that don't seem important at the time but are extremely useful to us."

"Of course, I'm sorry. It's just all been such a shock."

"I understand. That's all we need for now. Can Constable Johnston get you anything?"

"No thank you. I'm fine now."

There was a knock on the door and Dr Saunders entered.

"Inspector, I hope I'm not interrupting. I thought you might like some refreshments."

"Not at all, Sir. We had just finished."

As the door closed behind them, Sarah turned to Dr Saunders.

"Don't let's go back to the others," begged Sarah as Constable Johnson shut the door behind them. "I really don't think I can face everyone."

"Let's go for a walk in the garden. We'll go out the back door, through the kitchen and then no one will follow us."

"Oh thank you, Uncle Eddie. You're so good to me. I don't know what I'd do without you."

They went through the kitchen and came out onto the kitchen garden and from there onto the lawn. They walked for several minutes in silence and sat on one of the benches scattered around the gardens. Sarah looked at Uncle Eddie.

"I can't believe it. Jeremy's dead and the Inspector thinks one of us murdered him. I mean murder. It's all so awful."

"Now, now." Uncle Eddie patted Sarah's arm. "We don't know that. The poor chap could have had a heart attack or something of that kind. These things do happen. Don't you worry, my dear. It's going to be alright." Uncle Eddie put his arm protectively round Sarah.

Chapter 4

The Chuckling Professor

"So, Inspector, Marie tells me you wanted to see me."

"Yes, Professor. It won't take long"

"No problem. You've got to go over everyone's story, haven't you. I must say I would come to Eddie's little soirees more often if I thought they were this lively. "

Inspector Harbury looked at the chuckling Professor and smiled.

The Professor went on.

"Not a very lively evening for this poor chap though. I didn't know him very well. My wife could probably tell you more about him. In fact you know my wife, Inspector she'll tell you everything you need to know and whole lot more that you don't."

The Inspector tactfully said nothing.

"Could you tell me your movements earlier today, Sir."

"Yes. I was working on a new research paper in the study practically all day. Patricia kept disturbing me and nagging me to get ready. We've been married for over 20 years and she still insists I need half the afternoon to get ready for a dinner party. Anyway she seemed more agitated than usual so I gave up in the end and went to get changed at about 5pm. In fact it must have been ten past five exactly," finished the Professor triumphantly, "because the old grandfather clock had just chimed and it always runs 10 minutes slow."

"Dr Saunders said he had the party for Sarah to help her settle back into Hisbury. He said if she didn't have something to do he thought she would begin to imagine something was wrong in the village. Did you think anything was wrong in the village?"

"Something wrong in Hisbury." The Professor looked astonished. "No, I mean I hadn't noticed anything. "

"Did you think your wife had noticed anything? Do you think she was worried about something?"

"Well, if I was on as many committees as she is, I'd be worried, I can tell you!"

"But you didn't think she was concerned about something to do with village affairs or anything else?"

"No, I don't think so Inspector."

The Inspector went on. "So you left the house at what time?"

"It must have been about 6.45."

"And you walked across to the Hall with your wife and Gemma Haines?"

"Well actually, no. I walked across with Gemma."

"And your wife?"

"Well after spending the whole afternoon telling me to get ready and that we were leaving at 6.45, she had gone on ahead and so I walked across with Gemma and we caught up with Patricia on the way and all went in together."

"Did your wife say what she had been doing, Sir?"

"Well no, not really. I stopped trying to understand why women do things a long time ago Inspector."

The Inspector laughed. "Perhaps you could ask your wife to come and see me, Professor."

"Of course Inspector. Good luck!" The Professor left the room chuckling.

* * * * * * * * * * * * * * * * *

Patricia Quentin was in her early forties, an imposing and attractive woman. She was tall and stood straight and confidently. She had been an actress when Professor Quentin had met her. He was twenty years older than her but they had loved each other and had been married within 6 months of their first meeting. She accepted the chair that Constable Johnson offered her and stared angrily at the Inspector.

"I suppose you have to talk to everyone but surely you don't think that I am involved in this affair?" she said coldly.

"As you say, Mrs Quentin. It is all routine but I'm afraid I need to talk to everyone."

"Inspector," Mrs Quentin recovered herself and smiled her most tolerant smile at Inspector Harbury. "I quite understand. Of course you must see everyone, even those who you know could not possibly be involved. I mean we contribute to the Police Foundation Annual Ball. I am on the Committee." Mrs Quentin's voice rose slightly.

"And we are very grateful for all your hard work, Mrs Quentin, is that not true, Constable?"

"Yes, Sir," Constable Johnson had difficulty suppressing a smile.

"At what time did you arrive this evening, Mrs Quentin?"

"It must have been about 7pm, Inspector."

"And you arrived with your husband and your

companion, Gemma Haines."

"Yes. Sarah and Edward met us at the door and we all went onto the terrace for a drink. We were all there when we heard Marie scream and we all went out into the hall together."

"Thank you Mrs Quentin. You've been very helpful."

Mrs Quentin rose to leave.

"Oh, just one more thing, Mrs Quentin," said the Inspector.

"Yes, Inspector?"

"Your husband tells me that you left before him and he that walked up to the Hall with Gemma Haines and they met you on the way."

"Inspector, I really don't see.."

"Mrs Quentin, every little detail may be important."

Mrs Quentin looked confused and sat down again. "Charlie's right. I did leave before them. I had to have a word with one of the gardeners and by the time I'd finished it was gone 6.45 and I thought I'd just start walking up to the Hall."

"Thank you , Mrs Quentin", the Inspector watched as

Mrs Quentin left the room shutting the door rather firmly behind her.

He turned to Johnson. "Send Ms Haines in, will you Johnson? And have a word with the gardener."

"Yes, Sir," Johnson looked at the Inspector approvingly. Johnson told Ms Haines that the Inspector was ready to see her and then went out into the garden in search of the gardener who he found unloading bedding plants from his truck.

"Evening Constable. What brings you here?"

"It's Mr Marchington, Fred. He's been killed."

"Well I'll be damned and here at the Hall. I never thought I'd live to see the day."

"You might be able to help us actually, Fred."

"I'll do what I can Constable. You know what I think of Dr Saunders. He's always been good to me so I'll do anything to save him any trouble."

"It's just that we've been asking everyone what they were doing today and Mrs Quentin told us she walked up to the hall a little earlier at about 6.45 to speak to you."

"She might have done. I'm sure if that's what she said, then that's what she did but she didn't see me. I've only just got back from the market and I left here at about 3 o'clock. You know how it is. I got talking and the time just goes. Mind you I wouldn't want to make things awkward for Mrs Quentin. She can be a slave driver and a bit strong in her opinions but she's a good woman at heart."

"Thanks, Fred. I'll let the Inspector know."

Chapter 5

Gemma Haines Has Her Say

Gemma Haines knocked on the door of the library and having entered sat down facing Inspector Harbury across the large oak table.

"Thank you for coming, Ms Haines. This won't take long. I just want to get an idea of what happened before.."

"The murder. It's all right Inspector. I assume that's why you're here and I know you need to talk to all of us." The Inspector tactfully said nothing. "I can't tell you much. I'd heard people talk about Jeremy but I'd never seen him before."

"So the first time you saw him was when you all rushed out into the hall after hearing Marie scream?"

"No Inspector. That was the first time I knew who he was, yes. The first time I saw him was earlier that evening when I saw Mrs Quentin talking to him by the pond." Gemma Haines was not an unattractive woman but the Inspector had always thought she had a hard face and as she uttered these words, he saw the reality of his musings all the more clearly. The malice in her voice shocked the Inspector.

"Are you sure that the man you saw by the pond was the

same as the man in the Hall?"

"Yes Inspector, I'm sure." She got up as if to go and then turned back. "I have the utmost respect for the Professor, Inspector. He has been good to me and Patricia has always been kind in her own way but I believe in telling the truth Inspector and that's what I've done." Before the Inspector could reply, Ms Haines opened the door, went through it and walked resolutely away from the astonished Inspector and past Johnson who was trying to enter the room as she left it.

"I spoke to the gardener, Sir"

"And?"

"Well, he is usually here on a Friday afternoon and often stays until late especially during the long evenings but today he went out to the market to get some new bedding plants and he met people and got chatting and he's only just got back. I caught him unloading the plants ready to plant tomorrow."

"Very interesting. Well done Johnson. Now if you could put the same work into a cup of tea, we'll make a Sergeant out of you yet."

"Yes, Sir," Johnson turned towards the door thinking that, despite his boss's original mind, he didn't have a very funny sense of humour.

"Oh and Johnson perhaps you could have a word with Marie at the same time."

"Oh yes, Sir. Of course, Sir." Johnson left the room importantly. Old Harbury wasn't a bad chap really, he thought and hurried off to the kitchen where he found Marie clearing up.

"Could I have a word, Marie," said Constable Johnson feeling very important to be conducting interviews on his own.

Marie sat down, sniffed and looked wearily at the Constable.

"If you could just tell me in your own words what happened this evening, Marie."

"I took the cocktails into the sitting room and then I went to get some more and it was when I was coming back from the kitchen that he was just lying there in the hallway. I screamed and dropped the tray and then everyone came running in."

"And he hadn't been in the hall when you had gone down to the kitchen?"

"No. I mean I would have seen him."

"Yes well thank you Marie. Make sure you come and see us if you think of anything that could help us."

"I will." Marie got up to carry on clearing up but Constable Johnson had thought of another question.

"And you didn't see anyone around when you went down to the kitchen or back up again?"

"No I mean well only Mrs James in the kitchen. She was finishing off preparing dinner."

"Thank you Marie." Constable Johnson withdrew with a defeated expression on his face.

Chapter 6

Murder Is Not Childish

The Inspector had been sitting for several moments deep in thought, trying to make sense of the evening's happenings when there was a knock on the door. Dr Saunders entered.

"Inspector, the Reverend is asking if he could be seen next. He apparently promised to pay a visit to an elderly parishioner on his way home tonight and wants to get going."

"Of course. Send him in."

Dr Saunders left and a few minutes later the Reverend entered.

"A terrible tragedy, Inspector. Thank you for seeing me so quickly." The Rev sat down.

"Not at all, Reverend."

"It's poor old Mrs Hargreaves. She has been suffering so much with her Rheumatism and being a fellow sufferer myself I like to think I can be that little bit more understanding. Now how can I help?"

"Well, if you could just tell me in your own words what happened."

"Yes of course, I came up to the Hall with my sister at about 7pm or just after. I think we were a little late. Friday is a very busy day. I usually do a lot of visiting on a Friday. And then the rest I suspect you know. We were all having drinks, heard poor Marie scream and went into the Hall to find that poor boy just lying there."

"Reverend. you know everyone in the Parish well. It would help me so much to have the opinion of a man of your standing. Have you noticed anything unusual lately?"

The Reverend. drew himself up in his chair, easily flattered by the Inspector's words. "Well, of course, Mrs Quentin has been rather flustered lately, but then she is involved in so many charitable organisations, she is so busy. And, of course, my sister hasn't been the same since her husband died. She seemed to get better and then since the letters, she really has gone downhill."

"Letters?"

"Oh, I've told her it's a silly prank but it seems to have made her very jumpy."

"What exactly did the letters say, Reverend?"

"Oh the usual. "I'm watching you", "Don't do anything silly." So childish. Like something out of a detective novel."

"Murder is not childish, Reverend."

"No of course not but the letters are nothing to do with that."

"Well, thank you Reverend. Perhaps you could ask your sister to come in. I do hope Mrs Hargreaves is feeling better."

"Yes, yes, of course, Mrs Hargreaves." The Reverend hurried off.

* * * * * * * * * * * * * * * *

There was a timid knock at the door. The Inspector crossed the room to open it.

"Inspector, my brother said you asked to see me."

"Yes Mrs Woodgrove. Please do sit down. I just need you to tell me what happened this evening."

"It's all so horrible. Poor boy."

"Of course, Mrs Woodgrove, I understand it's been a very distressing evening but if there is anything you can tell us that may be of use."

"I'm sorry Inspector, I hardly knew Mr Marchington."

"Your brother told us that you had received some letters, Mrs Woodgrove?"

"Raif told you? Yes. He said I was being silly and that it was all a silly joke. He told me to throw them away and he was probably right but it's still a little unsettling. I got another one yesterday morning. Here, it's in my handbag. I didn't want Raif to find it. I kept the envelope as well. But they can't be connected to this. As I said I hardly knew Jeremy. "

The door opened suddenly and Mrs Woodgrove jumped as Constable Johnson entered the room.

"I'm sorry Inspector, I think this whole business has made me feel very on edge."

"Yes of course Mrs Woodgrove. Constable, perhaps you could make sure Mrs Woodgrove gets home safely and get this looked at." He gave the letter to Constable Johnson.

"Don't worry, Ma'am, we'll get to the bottom of this. If you think of anything else that I should know, you know where we are."

"Of course, Inspector. Thank you."

Constable Johnson opened the door for Mrs Woodgrove and they almost collided with Patrick Foley who had been just about to knock.

"Sorry Inspector, I didn't mean to barge in. Should I come back later?"

"No, Sir, we may as well talk now. Did you have something particular you wanted to tell me?"

"Well that's just it really. I don't have anything to tell you and it's been an exhausting evening. I promised to walk Sarah home."

"Particularly exhausting for Mr Marchington I would think, Sir."

"Well yes or course but I mean I didn't even see poor old Jeremy this evening, none of us did. I mean none of us knew him really well except Sarah and Eddie and even then only through Amanda. Everyone knows she was really sweet on him but there doesn't seem to be anything serious between them, not on his side anyway. Lord knows why. Sarah says a woman like Amanda will never settle and that she loves being the centre of attention but I think Amanda is simply lovely and I'm sure if she found the right man." Patrick looked wistfully off into the distance.

"Well thank you, Mr Foley. I'll come back with you to the sitting room. I do need to speak to Amanda and her companion."

The Inspector followed Patrick back to the sitting room

and they entered together. Everyone turned towards the Inspector.

"I do hope you've come to tell us we can all go home now, Inspector," said Patricia Quentin before the Inspector had a chance to say anything.

"Yes Mrs Quentin, I don't see why not. However, I must ask you all to keep yourselves available. We may need to speak to you again."

"Oh do come along Charles." Mrs Quentin swept out of the room followed by Professor Quentin who winked mischievously at the Inspector.

"I am going to walk Sarah home, Inspector. I won't be long," said Uncle Eddie and he left with Sarah. Patrick looked stood for a moment looking a little lost and then followed them out.

"Teddy be a darling and get me a drink," said Amanda. Teddy glanced at the Inspector and then at Amanda and left the room.

"Now he's gone, Inspector, we can talk properly. How can I help you?"

"I will need to speak to everyone, Ma'am."

"Oh Teddy won't be able to tell you anything. He's a darling but he doesn't notice anything."

"Did you notice anything that might help us this evening, Ms Cooper?"

"Well, it was all pretty usual. Sarah's a darling, of course and Eddie's very sweet for inviting me. Everyone else I don't know that well but I do know what they think of me. The Professor and the Reverend. are always very attentive, and Patrick is always there to get me a drink but I've heard the things Patricia says, she doesn't approve of me and Julia and Gemma wouldn't dare disagree with her."

"How well did you know Mr Marchington?"

"Jeremy? Well he was well known in the society pages, Inspector, but I actually met him at one of Edward's dos. He really is...was..." The door opened and Teddy walked over to Amanda and handed her a Martini. She took a long drink.

"I can't quite believe he's dead, Inspector. I mean he's broken a few hearts but I can't think of anyone who would really want to harm him."

Teddy stood in the shadows and glowered at Amanda.

"Can you tell me anything about today's events, Mr ..er..," the Inspector fixed his gaze on Teddy.

"As I said Inspector, Teddy hardly knew Jeremy."

"My name's Fielding, Inspector, Edward Fielding. Amanda's right I didn't know Jeremy well. I only met him through her and her friends but I knew enough to know that he wasn't the saint everyone thought he was."

"Teddy, please." Amanda gasped.

"What do you mean by that, Mr Fielding?"

"I mean that you can't go around stringing people along and expect them to hang on your every word." He turned and left the room slamming the door behind him.

"I'm sorry, Inspector, Teddy is not normally like that. He's a little too fond of me and very protective." Amanda smiled at the Inspector. "He never really approved of Jeremy."

"And you and Mr Marchington were good friends?"

Amanda paused and seemed to be studying the Inspector. She gave a strained laugh.

"Yes, Inspector, when Jeremy was in one place long enough to spend time with we got on. Now, if you don't have any further questions, it's been a long day and I would like to go back to London."

"Of course, Ms Cooper. If you could just make sure that Constable Johnson has your details in case we need to contact you."

"Of course, Inspector." Amanda got up and left the room.

The Inspector sat still for a moment and did not hear Constable Johnson come in.

"Judge Seagrave is asking if you will see him now, Sir."

"Of course. Show him in would you, Constable."

"So, Inspector I hear you have left me until last."

"Last but by no means least Judge." The Inspector smiled wearily at the Judge who he knew well as he lived locally and they had come into contact many times through cases they had both worked on.

"Well let's get it over with. I'm normally tucked up in bed by now."

"You know the drill, Sir. What were your movements today? How well did you know the deceased? Is there anything you can tell us that could help with our enquiries?"

"This morning I read the papers and then did some work on a case that I've been asked my opinion on. Very interesting as it happens. Murder case but the defence want to plead temporary insanity. Apparently the girl is outwardly perfectly normal but out of the blue she attacked and killed this man and then had no recollection of what she'd done. Of course very difficult to prove. She could be putting it on but hard to convince a professional psychiatrist. Anyway that took me to lunch time and then I had to go up to town for a dentist appointment. By the time I got back Patrick was hurrying me to get ready for the party. I think he was keen to see Sarah." The Judge smiled. "I just hope she says yes to him or he'll be unbearable. You know Inspector that's why I never married. Altogether too much effort. I mean look what happened to the poor girl my younger brother took up with. She falls in love, he gets her into trouble and then runs out on her and she can't bring up a child on her own and so I'm left with young Patrick. Still he seems to have turned out alright."

"I completely agree with you, Sir. I am quite happy coming home to my pipe and old Rover. The thing about dogs is they never contradict you."

"Quite so. Anyway where were we? Oh yes, Jeremy. I wouldn't say I knew him well. We moved in similar circles and had some mutual friends like Eddie but apart from that. We were not what I would call close."

"Thank you, Sir. If you think of anything else. I mean we're always happy to have the benefit of your experience."

"Of course. Keep me informed and if you need someone

to share ideas with, feel free to drop by."

"Thank you, Sir. I will."

"Goodnight Harbury."

"Goodnight, Sir."

The Judge left the room and a few moments later Constable Johnson came in.

"I've taken down everyone's details, Sir. I saw Ms Cooper as she left you. She's a cool customer, that one, Sir, and no mistake."

"I think you're right there Constable, I think you're right. By the way, did you learn anything from Marie?"

"No, nothing new, Sir. I told her to come and see us if she thinks of anything, however small it seems."

"Good. Well, I think we've done all we can this evening. We'll come down here at first light and take a proper look outside and I will send Constable Braddon round to Mr Marchington's flat tonight to secure it."

Chapter 7

Mrs Quentin Has A Headache

Patricia Quentin lay back on the couch in the drawing room holding a cold compress to her head.

"Gemma, Darling, you couldn't pass me my shawl. I really can't move with this headache. Thank you, dear and could you remind the Professor that we promised to visit the Hall for afternoon tea. I really would rather not go this afternoon but one has to be supportive of Eddie. Poor dear. What a very trying evening and before he'd even served dinner."

Gemma got up and brought the shawl to Patricia who sat up slightly and allowed Gemma to place it on her shoulders.

"Dear Gemma, I don't know what I'd do without you." Patricia laid a hand on Gemma's arm.

Gemma smiled and looking a little awkward turned towards the door and walked out in the direction of the Professor's study.

As Gemma walked out of the room, the Professor strolled in through the veranda doors. He went silently up to Patricia, who was still lying with the compress on and kissed her on the top of the head.

"Oh, Charles, you made me jump. What were you doing out there? I thought you were in your study. "

"I was but it's such a lovely morning I thought I would go for a stroll. Besides, I thought some fresh air might clear my head after last night's antics." The Professor chuckled. "Don't I always tell you I'd be better off in my study. If people read more instead of insisting on socialising so much, things like this would never happen. I mean a book never killed anyone."

"Believe me Darling, that can be arranged!" Patricia gave her husband's hand a squeeze. "Sit with me a while Charlie, this is all so horrible."

Professor Quentin sat on the edge of the sofa and took his wife's hand.

"I know, Darling, but you've got nothing to worry about. It's nothing to do with us. I hardly knew Jeremy and you knew him from years ago but you only saw him occasionally at Eddie's and he's a nice enough chap. Why should we want to do him any harm?"

"Inspector Harbury and Constable Johnston, Ma'am," a neatly dressed, young parlourmaid, having knocked timidly and got no response, opened the door and stepped into the room.

"Oh thank you, Rose. We can see them in here."

"Yes Ma'am. Ma'am, the Inspector asked if Professor Quentin would show the Constable which way you usually walk up to the Hall."

"Why on earth.." Mrs Quentin started.

"Don't worry, Patricia, it's all routine. I'll show the Constable now and perhaps you could get the Inspector some tea, Rose."

"Yes, Sir."

The Professor left with Rose in search of the Constable and a few moments later Inspector Harbury entered the room.

"Good morning, Mrs Quentin. I am sorry to disturb you. Would you like me to come back when you are feeling better?" he motioned towards the compress.

"Thank you Inspector but no it is just a slight headache. What can I do for you?"

"Well ma'am it's really a question of following up enquiries you understand. We have to investigate all the information we have been given."

"Well of course, Inspector. I will help you in every way I can but I really don't see what else I can tell you."

"You were seen earlier yesterday evening talking with Mr Marchington. Could you tell me what you were talking about. You understand, that if Mr Marchington was in the area before the dinner party, it may provide us with a lead."

Mrs Quentin's white face showed that the Inspector had hit a nerve, but she kept her composure beautifully.

"Oh, did I not mention that Inspector? Yes I saw Jeremy briefly. "

"Was it a chance meeting, Mrs Quentin?"

"Inspector, why would I arrange to meet someone that I was going to see in half an hour's time?"

"At about what time did you meet Mr Marchington?"

"Well, as I said I went across to see the gardener and.."

"The gardener tells us that he went into market yesterday evening, Ma'am and didn't get back until late."

"Yes, well I got talking to Jeremy and didn't manage to see the gardener and then realising the time I walked up to the Hall."

"How did you meet Mr Marchington, Ma'am?"

"I've known Jeremy for years, Inspector. We don't see

each other much now except when he comes down for one of Eddie's parties. I'm afraid I don't know anything that can help you."

"If you remember anything else please do let us know. I assure you that anything you tell us will be kept in strictest confidence."

"Inspector, I don't appreciate what you are implying."

"Mrs Quentin, you knew the deceased for many years and anything that you know about his life could help us." The Inspector paused but Mrs Quentin sat in silence. "Well, Ma'am, if you remember anything that you think would be of help to us, you know where we are."

Professor Quentin appeared through the veranda doors.

"Ah, Inspector, I've showed your Constable everything he wanted to know.
Are we any closer to clearing this up?" said Professor Quentin in a much more jovial voice than the subject matter would usually require or his grave eyes implied.

"Well, thank you Professor, Mrs Quentin. I'll be in touch."

The Inspector turned and left the room and Professor Quentin sat back down next to his wife.

Patricia looked at her husband. "You look tired, Darling.

Maybe you should have a lie down. I'll come up and tell you myself when lunch is ready."

"Is everything all right? I saw the Inspector leaving." Sarah stood in the doorway.

"Yes dear," Patricia Quentin smiled at her daughter. "It was just all such a shock. Jeremy was a very old friend and it's awful to think that someone would want to harm him like that."

"I know," said Sarah, "but things are in good hands with Inspector Harbury."

Inspector Harbury walked out onto the drive and was met by Constable Johnson. "Is the car ready, Constable? I want to catch the next train to London. I sent Constable Braddon up last night to keep an eye on Mr Marchington's flat and make sure nothing was disturbed but I want to look at the place myself."

"Yes, Sir. Everything's ready. Constable Braddon has reported quite an eventful morning."

Chapter 8

Inspector Harbury's Tea

Constable Braddon had got a call from Inspector Harbury late on the evening of the murder requesting that he go upto London first thing in the morning, straight to the deceased's flat, seal it and make sure that no-one disturbed anything until Inspector Harbury joined him.

He had followed his instructions efficiently and had reached and entered the flat with no problem using the keys found on the deceased. Having entered the flat Constable Braddon had taken a thorough look around to make sure it was empty and that the windows and doors were secure. He had then made himself a cup of tea and sat on a chair next to the telephone table in the entrance hall. Having been accepted into the police force due to his quick learning and hard work, rather than his love of early mornings, Constable Braddon was soon dozing peacefully.

True to his training, the ordinary sound of the grandfather clock did not wake him but with the noise of a key turning in the lock of the front door, he stirred and sat alert and waiting. The telephone table was obscured by a coat rack that stood just inside the front door and so Constable Bradden's chair was partially hidden. This and the fact that the small panes of glass in the top of the front door did not let much light in meant that the hall was badly lit. The figure entered, made its way down the hall and turned into the living room. Constable Bradden got up and followed the intruder along the hall. When he reached the living room door, he suddenly turned on the light. The figure swung round and in his surprise tripped over a small coffee table and fell to the floor. Constable Bradden took his chance and jumped forward and seized his prisoner.

"All right, take it easy. Let's not make this worse. What do you think you're doing crossing a police line?" And then suddenly, catching a glimpse of the intruder's face for the first time, "Mr Foley. What on earth..." His surprise at seeing Patrick momentarily took him away from his duty but he soon recovered himself. "I think you should come with me, Sir. The Inspector will want to ask you a few questions."

Patrick looked white and tired. "I...I can explain," he stammered.

The Constable, who had been posted in Hisbury for the past few years, had always found Patrick welcoming and friendly. He was the last person the Constable would have expected to be taking to the station.

When Inspector Harbury and Constable Johnson arrived in London there was a police car waiting for them. They were told about Patrick and made their way to the police station near Mr Marchington's flat instead of to the flat itself, which now stood empty.

The sorry sight that greeted Inspector Harbury in the interview room would have been enough to soften the heart of a much harder man.

"Good morning, Mr Foley."

"I wouldn't say that, Inspector," said Patrick with just the flicker of a smile on his pale, tired face and barely a trace of the usual sparkle in his eyes.

"Constable, perhaps you could rustle up some tea for Mr Foley and I wouldn't say no to a cup either."

Constable Johnson left the room leaving the Inspector and Constable Braddon with Mr Foley. The Inspector sat down opposite Mr Foley.

"Now I think you've got some explaining to do Mr Foley."

"I know it looks bad, Inspector, but I assure you that there is a perfectly reasonable explanation, well I mean I don't know if it's reasonable exactly but it's the truth."

"Go on."

"When we heard Marie's scream at the party yesterday, we all rushed into the hall but I was just ahead of everyone and I found this." Patrick held out a small silver broach shaped like a butterfly.

The Inspector took a handkerchief out of his pocket and laid the broach on it. "Constable get this looked at will you. Although I should think the chance of finding any valuable prints on it now is unlikely."

"I know I should have told you straight away but it's Sarah's broach. I don't know how it could have got there but it wasn't her. I mean it couldn't have been her, Inspector. Sarah would never do anything like this and besides, she wasn't wearing that broach last night. I remember, she was wearing a silver pendent and the earrings I bought her for her last birthday but no broach. It must have been planted. I suppose I thought that I might find some answers to all of this in Jeremy's flat."

"Did you tell anyone else about this, Mr Foley?"

"No, I didn't tell anyone. I just thought I might find something useful - a lead."

"And where did you get the key from?"

"Dr Saunders has had one for ages. Jeremy was away a lot and Dr Saunders doesn't come to London as much as he used to. He sold his London flat a few years ago and now he stays in hotels or uses Jeremy's flat. I borrowed the key last night before I left. It's hanging in the key box in the hall. You know Hisbury, Inspector. It's a small community. No one feels the need to keep things like that locked up." He paused. "Well not until yesterday."

There was knock at the door and Constable Johnson entered.

"I hadn't realised that tea was so hard to come by, Constable."

"I'm sorry, Sir but it's Mr Marchington's flat. A neighbour has reported hearing broken glass. It looks like there's been a break-in."

"You see, Inspector." Patrick jumped up in excitement. "There was something in that flat."

"Yes, Sir, something which by now is long gone because I've been sitting here talking to you."

"I'm sorry, Inspector. From now on anything I learn I'll come straight to you." He paused. "I don't suppose I can tag along to the flat. I've been there to Jeremy's parties. I might be able to help - you know notice if something is missing."

"Mr Foley, I would have thought you'd had enough excitement for one day." Inspector Harbury relented. "All right but you do not touch anything without my say-so."

"Of course."

"Constable Bradden, let's get going. Constable Johnson,

where is the tea?"

"But, Sir.."

The Inspector left the room listening to Constable Johnson's protests. Constable Bradden and Patrick followed behind them, Patrick looking a bit more like his old self. In spite of the recent events, he felt excited at the prospect of helping with the case. At least now they had a lead.

Chapter 9

The Constable Meets His Match

Ten minutes later the four men had reached Jeremy Marchington's flat and Constable Johnson had relieved the duty officer and taken up his position standing just outside the front door to ensure that no-one no one came in. The Inspector went into the living room with Constable Bradden and Patrick.

"Well it all looks the same down here, Sir," said Constable Bradden."Let's take a look upstairs. The duty officer first on the scene said one of the upstairs bedrooms appeared to be the only room which was disturbed. Whoever broke in obviously knew what they were looking for."

"What about the overturned coffee table in here, Constable? Did nobody mention that?"

"Well actually, Inspector, I knocked that over earlier today." Patrick went a little red at the mention of the morning's antics.

"Right then, let's take a look upstairs." Inspector Harbury motioned to Constable Bradden to lead the way.

On reaching the landing, Constable Bradden led the two men into a bedroom which in turn led onto a small study. Both rooms where in disarray. The drawers from the chest in the bedroom had been pulled out and their contents overturned and strewn all over the bed and the rest of the room. The wardrobe contents were in the same state and even the bed mattress was askew as if someone had thought whatever they were seeking could be hidden there. The trail of clothes and possessions led into the study where the mayhem continued. Papers had been pulled out from the desk drawers and carelessly dropped, presumably when the intruder saw they were useless.

"Well, our intruder was certainly in a hurry to find something." The Inspector turned to Constable Bradden. "Has anyone seen the neighbour who reported this yet?"

"No Sir, I'll get onto that now." They were interrupted by a woman's voice downstairs.

"I've been coming here every Wednesday and Friday for the past ten years and keeping house for Mr Marchington, my lad and I've not intention of letting him down. He's a good man."

"That sounds like someone who may be able to help us. Constable, while I'm with her, you can speak to the neighbour and get a fingerprinting team down here."

"Yes, Sir."

Constable Bradden went out of the room and the Inspector held the door open for Patrick, as if making sure he left the room and they went downstairs.

Constable Johnson was still trying to pacify Mr Marchington's housekeeper, whose raised voice had suggested a much larger person. In reality Mrs Campbell was a small lady, with greying hair tied back in a bun. However, what she lacked in physical proportions, she made up for in character. Years of hard work had made her robust and she was proving quite a challenge for the gentle Constable Johnson.

The Inspector stepped forward and introductions were made.

"Thank you. Constable. I'll take it from here." Inspector Harbury turned to the now dewy eyed Mrs Campbell. "If you'd like to come into the living room Mrs Campbell, I would like to ask you a few questions."

"Of course, Inspector. I'll help you in any way I can. He was a good man."

"Thank you Mrs Campbell," and turning to Constable Johnson. "Perhaps you could get Mrs Campbell a cup of tea, Constable."

"Thank you, Inspector. You're very kind."

The Inspector sat opposite Mrs Campbell and studied the kindly face whose eyes looked intelligently back at him.

"How long have you been working for Mr Marchington, Mrs Campbell?"

"Almost ten years, Sir. My sister used to work for him but she moved away and she put in a good word for me and Mr Marchington was happy to take me on and we got on well and I stayed. He was always good to me, Sir. I can't think who would do something so terrible."

"So there is no-one you know who Mr Marchington had any problems with in the past?"

Mrs Campbell looked reluctant.

"This is all in the strictest confidence you understand," Inspector Harbury added. "It's just that you've been in a very valuable position, Mrs Campbell. Working for someone for such a long time in their home, you could not help but notice anything unusual and you could not help overhearing if any unpleasantness occurred or if on any occasion Mr Marchington seemed worried by something. However small it seems, it could help us."

"Well, Sir, now I think about it, there was one thing. I thought it odd at the time but you don't dwell on these things, do you? I mean it's not my business. He was always good to me, wages on time and a good bonus at Christmas. I don't think it's proper to go wondering about other people's affairs."

"What was it you noticed, Mrs Campbell?"

"Well, Sir, it started about two months ago. Mr Marchington received a letter. It seemed to trouble him, Sir. I remember because he didn't finish his morning tea. I always bring him his tea on the days I'm here and there was that letter lying on the mat, which was odd because Mr Marchington usually collected the early morning mail before I arrived. He opened it and then he went straight out and didn't even drink his tea and it was his favourite homemade oatmeal and raisin biscuits, made fresh that morning."

"And did you happen to notice where the letter was posted from, Mrs Campbell?"

"Well that was peculiar too, Sir. It was addressed but it had no stamp on it. Whoever it was must have pushed it through the letter box themselves."

"And you don't know where Mr Marchington went that day?"

"Well, Sir, I leave just after lunch and he wasn't back by then but I came in the next day that week as I was having Friday off for the christening of my sister's new baby and he asked me to take his tweed jacket to the cleaners. I checked the pockets and found a train ticket to Hisbury dated the day before."

"And did you notice anything unusual after this?"

"He had a visitor one day. I usually answer the door when I'm here but he had said he was expecting someone and he'd look after them. I didn't see who it was but I was in the kitchen and the living room door was ajar. I couldn't hear much of what was being said except that it seemed to be a woman's voice. The only thing I heard was when Mr Marchington raised his voice once. I remembered because he was usually so good-natured. "You can't do this. I won't allow it," he said and then it went quiet again."

"Did the woman stay long?"

"No, Sir. Not long."

"And it wasn't a voice you recognised?"

"No, Sir."

"Was this the only time she visited that you know of."

"Yes, Sir."

"Thank you, Mrs Campbell. If you wouldn't mind waiting, I would like you to take a look at the bedroom and the study once we have finished in there and let us know if you notice anything missing."

"Yes of course, Sir. You'll catch whoever did this won't you, Inspector?"

"We'll do our best, Mrs Campbell."

* * * * * * * * * * * * * * * * *

While the Inspector was talking to Mrs Campbell, Constable Braddon took the opportunity to go and speak to the neighbour who had reported the break-in. The door was opened by a young woman holding a baby.

"Good morning, Ma'am. Sorry to disturb you but my name is Constable Bradden. You reported a break-in next door this morning?"

"Yes I did, Constable. I heard breaking glass from the back of the house and when I came outside onto our patio, I saw someone putting their arm through the broken pane of the back door and going into the house."

"Did you see their face, Ma'am?"

"No I didn't see their face but it was definitely a woman, tall, brown hair and she wore a brown skirt and a little black jacket and a black cap which looked quite odd as if she was trying to hide her face."

* * * * * * * * * * * * * * * * *

"So it looks like they didn't find what they were looking for, Sir."

"Well, either they didn't find what they were looking for

or they found it and Mrs Campbell just didn't notice it was missing or didn't know of its existence."

Having left Constable Bradden at the flat, Inspector Harbury and Constable Johnson were in a taxi heading back to the station where Inspector Harbury put a call through to the pathologist.

"Hi Tommy. Any news on the Marchington case?"

"Well it's funny you should call. I was just about to ring you. Mr Marchington was poisoned, more specifically he died of Glyphosate poisoning or to the layman he ingested weedkiller. I would say that poison cases are usually premeditated but with this kind of poison, not necessarily. It's readily available in most households."

"And time of death?"

"Now that's the really interesting bit. He hadn't been dead more than a couple of hours when I attended him but it was a couple of hours."

"How could he have died a couple of hours ago when he wasn't in the hall when people were coming through less than half an hour before?"

"That's your department. I'm just telling you when I believe he was killed."

"Thanks Tommy. At least that narrows down the time

but it does mean that anyone could have killed him but how on earth he suddenly appeared in the hall, I have no idea."

"That's why I became a pathologist and not an Inspector. Reading dead bodies is easy but finding out how they came to be in that state is beyond me."

The Inspector rang off.

Chapter 10

Mayhew and Pickering

Inspector Harbury and Constable Johnson were in a taxi heading for Lincoln's Inn Fields and the offices of Messrs Mayhew, Mayhew and Pickering, Solicitors to the late Jeremy Marchington.

They sat silently for several minutes and then Inspector Harbury spoke. "Well let's hope Mr Mayhew can shed some light on this case. What with dead bodies appearing out of nowhere when all the suspects are having drinks in the next room, I think we need a little help. At least he should be able to tell us who benefits from Mr Marchington's death."

Having arrived at the solicitors, Inspector Harbury and Constable Johnson were greeted by a smart looking young woman and shown into a small waiting room.

"Mr Mayhew will not be long, Gentleman. He's just finishing a telephone call," said the young woman and her perfectly polished nails resumed their typing.

"Thank you." The Inspector sat down on one of the expensive looking leather armchairs and picked up the coffee that had been placed on the coffee table next to him.

The coffee was still piping hot and the clock struck

12.00 as Mr Mayhew left his desk, walked across his office, through another door into his secretary's office and a young man appeared in the waiting room where Inspector Harbury and Constable Johnson were sitting.

"Gentleman, I do hope I haven't kept you waiting."

"Not at all, Sir."

The Inspector and Constable Johnson were ushered into Mr Mayhew's office and their coffee reappeared beside them.

"Mr Harbury, isn't it. What can I do for you, Sir? My secretary tells me it's something of the utmost confidentiality. I can assure you that the firm of Mayhew, Mayhew and Pickering is known for its discretion."

"Thank you, Mr Mayhew. It's Inspector, actually. I'm afraid we've got some bad news for you concerning one of your clients."

Inspector Harbury told Mr Mayhew about Mr Marchington's demise and while he was talking he couldn't help but notice that the solicitor's face betrayed little emotion.

"I'm sorry to hear that, Inspector. I will of course try to help you in any way that I can. I'm afraid I cannot boast a long relationship with the deceased. My father dealt with Mr Marchington's affairs for twenty years until he recently retired. I am sure that he would be of much greater help to you than I can. As well as employing him to deal with any legal matters, Mr Marchington considered him a close friend."

"Would it be possible for us to speak with your father?"

"Yes it could be arranged. He is elderly and gets tired easily but his memory is still excellent. I will ask my secretary to give you his telephone number and address."

"Thank you, Sir. Is it possible to also tell us who benefits from Mr Marchington's death?"

"I can find that information for you, Inspector but I must also tell you that when Mr Marchington came to see me recently on routine matters, he mentioned that he wished to draft a new will. He did not ask my advice on content but merely said that he would send the draft to me. I could then draw up the new will and he would come in and sign it."

"What did the new will contain, Mr Mayhew?"

Mr Mayhew's face became grave. "I'm afraid I have not heard from Mr Marchington since then, Inspector."

"And the will you currently hold?"

"Well, Inspector, after my recent conversation with Mr

Marchington I had a quick look at the file. Mr Marchington had no close family. His parents had passed away and he had no brothers or sisters. The will contains various charity bequests, a small annuity for a Mrs Campbell, who I believe kept house for him, and a small proportion of his estate was to be settled on a maiden aunt. However, the bulk of the estate, which even after death duties will be considerable, is left in full to a Mrs Patricia Quentin, with the rather unnecessary codicil that she should be informed with the utmost confidentiality."

"Did Mr Marchington's manner seem at all unusual to you when you last saw him, Mr Mayhew?"

"I would not have said so, Inspector. He was grave but then he took his business affairs very seriously. I did not think he was troubled by anything in particular. As I said, the only comment I would make is that he did not consult me on the drafting of his new will. He was obviously quite sure of the changes he wished to make."

"Thank you, Mr Mayhew. One last thing. If I could have a copy of the will you currently hold and if you think of anything else that may help us, please do get in touch."

"Of course, Inspector. If you wait in the reception, I will ask my secretary to bring you the papers you need."

Having said their goodbyes to Mr Mayhew, Inspector Harbury and Constable Johnson were left in the capable hands of his secretary. This time the smart woman seemed distracted and Inspector Harbury noticed that her eyes were suspiciously red. Miss Monroe, as the plaque on her desk indicated, busied herself preparing the papers that the Inspector had asked for. Once that was done and the Inspector was preparing to leave she suddenly spoke.

"Is it really true about Mr Marchington, Inspector?"

"I'm afraid so, Miss," the Inspector paused. "Did you know the deceased well?"

"Not very well, Sir. He invited me out to dinner a few weeks ago and he was nice. I hoped we would go out again."

"Did he mention anything to you that could help us understand why he was killed?"

Miss Monroe sniffed noisily. The Inspector handed her his handkerchief.

"Thank you, Inspector. I'm sorry but he was such a nice man. He was so attentive, took my coat at the restaurant and opened the door for me. I can't imagine why anyone would want to harm him."

The Inspector nodded sympathetically and then continued with his questioning. "Did Mr Marchington say anything about changing his will?"

"I knew he was going to. I mean it's not a very big office and it's easy to overhear people and of course Mr Mayhew made a note on the file that we should make another appointment for Mr Marchington when he rang."

There was a pause and then Miss Monroe said. "He did mention one thing. I said thank you for a lovely evening. I must admit I hoped that he might want to go out again. Then he said we would get together again soon and I was glad and said that would be lovely. It was then that he suddenly looked kind of serious and said there was something he had to sort out first, something out of town."

"Thank you, Miss Monroe. If you think of anything else, please do contact us." Having given Miss Monroe one of his cards, the Inspector left the office of Messrs Mayhew, Mayhew and Pickering. Constable Johnson hailed a taxi to take them back the police station, where it transpired that nothing of interest had been found so far at Mr Marchington's flat. This done, Constable Johnson made a telephone call and was soon accompanying Inspector Harbury to South London to call on Mr Mayhew Senior.

It didn't take long before the car was driving through a leafy residential area of London and drew up in front of a smart looking apartment block. Constable Johnson parked the car and he and Inspector Harbury went into the building. They entered the lift and soon found themselves outside number 32. A smart looking nurse opened the door and ushered them into a large room at the back of the apartment. An elderly man sat in a wheelchair. He was very small and frail but his eyes were shrewd and intelligent and when he spoke his voice was much stronger than you would have expected. The Inspector suddenly had an image of Mr Mayhew Senior as a much younger man sitting in the offices of Mayhew, Mayhew and Pickering efficiently dealing with the legal matters of the day. The Inspector felt sure he would have been a force to be reckoned with.

All this went through the Inspector's mind as he entered the room and then introductions were made and he sat on the sofa opposite Mr Mayhew and Constable Johnson sat on a chair a little way away and got out his notebook.

Mr Mayhew opened the conversation. "My son telephoned me and told me about Jeremy. He was a good man. I would like to do everything I can to help you, Inspector."

"Thank you Mr Mayhew. Your son told me that as well as dealing with Mr Marchington's legal affairs, you considered him a close friend."

"Yes, Inspector. I had known Jeremy for many years."

"Was there anything you can tell me about his life that could help us to know who may want to harm him?"

Mr Mayhew smiled. "Jeremy lived life to the full,

Inspector. He enjoyed his life and that included the company of women but he made no secret of the fact that he was not the settling down type."

"And you know of no-one that bore him a grudge?"

"No, Inspector."

"Your son told us that Patricia Quentin was the chief benefactor of Jeremy's will. Do you know why that was?"

Mr Mayhew paused before answering. "It was a long time ago, Inspector, but I believe there was something between them and then Patricia met the Professor and had Sarah."

"And they remained friends?"

"I never heard anything to the contrary."

"Your son also told us that Mr Marchington had mentioned he wanted to make a new will but did not discuss any changes with him before he died. Do you have any idea what changes he would have wanted to make?"

"No, Inspector although I am surprised that his will still left everything to Patricia. It seems a change was long overdue."

"And there is nothing else you can tell us?"

"No, Inspector. I am so very sorry. I fear I have not been of much help to you."

"Not at all, Sir. Thank you for your time."

Having thanked Mr Mayhew Senior, Inspector Harbury and Constable Johnson made their way to the train station and were soon sitting in a warm train compartment heading towards Hisbury and eating a much deserved lunch while they reviewed the case.

"So, Constable what do you think?"

"Well, Sir," said Constable Johnson, pleased that his boss wanted to know what he thought. "It seems that Mrs Quentin had quite a motive. Mr Marchington left her everything in his will."

"Yes we will need to speak to Mrs Quentin again to find out why Mr Marchington would leave everything to her but from what I can see she wasn't in need of the money." Harbury paused and thoughtfully chewed his sandwich. "One thing I would like to know Constable is why Mr Marchington was planning to change his will. It might be worth us speaking to everyone again with this new information and seeing how they react."

"And what about Miss Quentin, Sir? That's the bit that puzzles me the most, Sir. We found her broach by Mr

Marchington's body and then there is the ear-ring that we found at Mr Marchington's flat that Patrick identified as being Sarah's. She always seemed such a nice lady to me. I can't believe she could be mixed up in this."

"I find it hard to believe as well Constable but you can't get away from the facts. And you never know what people will do for money. Perhaps she knew her mother was going to inherit and knew that Jeremy was going to change his will. Perhaps Jeremy knew something about her that she didn't want to get out. Whatever the possible motive, after the evidence of the broach and the ear-ring, we definitely need to have a little chat."

Chapter 11

Afternoon Tea at the Hall

"Oh do come on, Darling. You know how I hate being late." Mrs Quentin's irritation sprung more from her frayed nerves after everything that had happened than anything else and Professor Quentin and Sarah rushed to pacify her and accompany her to the Hall for afternoon tea. Gemma was already waiting with Mrs Quentin. "I do hope it will just be the five of us," said Mrs Quentin. "I really don't feel like being around too many people this afternoon."

They set off across the garden and round to the front of the Hall. Marie opened the door to Professor Quentin's knock and told them that Dr Saunders was on the terrace and that she would bring tea now they had all arrived.

Mrs Quentin grimaced at the thought that their party was to be larger than she had hoped. She followed her husband onto the veranda where Sarah and Gemma had already greeted Dr Saunders and were settling themselves into the chintzy cushions of the wicker chairs around the coffee table. She was relieved to see that the only other visitor was Patrick. Dear Patrick. Such a pleasant young man.

"Patricia, my dear," Dr Saunders came towards her. "You look tired. Sit down and Marie will bring us some tea."

"Thank you, Eddie. I cannot seem to shake this headache. And of course the Inspector is asking questions all the time. It really is so trying."

"Of course, it's been a great shock to all of us." Dr Saunders sat down wearily in his chair.

Marie brought the tea and the party's spirits momentarily rose as they consumed sandwiches and large slices of home-made cake. Professor Quentin sat back contentedly in his chair and took a sip of tea.

"So Eddie, have you got anything else planned to keep us on our toes?"

"Charles, really. How could you." Patricia threw a mock reproachful look at her husband. Dr Saunders smiled at the Professor and took up the bait.

"Well, Charles it's funny you should mention this. I did think we should do something to take our minds off everything that's happened. What about a trip up to town? We could have dinner, take in a show?"

"Capital idea, Eddie. Perhaps if you take the girls off my hands I can get on with finishing this paper of mine."

"I would be only too delighted to escort two such beautiful women. I can't see why you would pass up the opportunity."

"You two really are terrible!" said Patricia looking affectionately at Dr Saunders and her husband. For the first time since Jeremy's death, the atmosphere felt lighter and more normal.

"Yes, Marie?" Dr Saunders noticed that Marie had returned and was waiting to speak to him.

"Sorry, Sir, but Inspector Harbury is here."

"Of course. Show him into the study."

"He says he wants to see Miss Quentin, Sir."

"What?" Sarah's voice trembled. "Why would he want to see me? I've told him everything I know. I mean there wasn't much to tell."

"It's all right Sarah dear. We'll sort this out. Show the Inspector in here please Marie. There's nothing that he's got to say that can't be said in front of all of us."

"Yes, Sir." Marie hurried out and a few seconds later reappeared with Inspector Harbury and Constable Johnson.

"I'm sorry to disturb you, Sir," Inspector Harbury addressed Dr Saunders.

"That's all very well Inspector but don't you think

Sarah's been through enough. She's told you everything she knows. You're barking up the wrong tree Inspector. None of us even saw Jeremy that day."

"I'm afraid we have evidence that we feel Miss Quentin could help us with. If you could accompany us to the station, Miss."

Dr Saunders sat down, deflated by the shock of the Inspector's words.

"This is outrageous Harbury," Professor Quentin looked menacingly at the Inspector.

"It's alright Daddy, really. There must be some mistake. I'll answer the Inspector's questions and I'm sure we can sort this out." Sarah followed Constable Johnson out of the room with the Inspector close behind them. Professor Quentin sank into his chair as Mrs Quentin began to sob quietly.

Chapter 12

Inspector Harbury Acts

Sarah sat opposite the Inspector and he couldn't help thinking that, despite the evidence, something didn't seem right. The look on her face was of complete disbelief but after what he had found what choice did he have. These thoughts ran quickly through the Inspector's mind and then he pulled himself together and brought himself back to the matter at hand.

"Thank you for coming to talk to us, Miss Quentin. Would you like a drink?"

"No thank you, Inspector." Sarah sat perfectly still waiting for the Inspector to continue.

"There are just a few questions that I need to ask you concerning some evidence that we have found."

Sarah's expression didn't change. In fact, thought Inspector Harbury, she showed no signs of knowing what he was talking about.

The Inspector put a plastic evidence bag in front of Sarah.

"Have you ever seen this broach?"

Sarah merely glanced at the broach. "Yes Inspector. It's

mine. I lost it recently. Where did you find it?"

"You are sure it's yours, Miss Quentin? Look closely."

Sarah bent forward and studied the broach. "Yes, it's definitely mine. I know because one of the little flowers is slightly worn."

"It was found next to Jeremy Marchington's body on the day he was murdered."

"And so you think I killed him?"

"We need to know how it came to be found next to Mr Marchington's body."

"I'm sorry Inspector but I can't help you. I lost the broach about a week ago. I had been at Uncle Eddie's that day and went back to look for it but I didn't find it. I just thought it would turn up."

"Have you ever been in Mr Marchington's flat, Miss Quentin?"

"I was there once when I was in London. Uncle Eddie lent me the key. Jeremy was away and Uncle Eddie didn't think he would mind."

The Inspector placed another item in front of Sarah. It was a gold earring.

"Is this your earring?"

"Yes, Inspector. It's mine. I had noticed it was missing but I couldn't remember where I had lost it. Where did you find it?"

"We found it in Jeremy Marchington's flat yesterday. Could you have left it when you were there?"

"I don't think so, Inspector. I'm sure I've worn those earrings since then. I just thought I'd lost it in Hisbury somewhere."

"So you can't give me any more information?"

"No, Inspector. Look people lose things, earrings, broaches, it happens all the time. I was upset that I had lost one of the earrings as Patrick had brought them for me. They weren't terribly valuable but they were pretty and I liked them."

"Do you know where in Hisbury you might have left it?"

Sarah looked straight at the Inspector. "If I had known where I'd left it Inspector, it wouldn't be lost."

Harbury had to concede she had a point.

* * * * * * * * * * * * * *

Inspector Harbury came out of the interview room to

discover that Professor and Mrs Quentin were waiting for him in reception.

"Show them into my office, Constable," said Inspector Harbury wearily.

Constable Johnson hurried off and Inspector Harbury went along the corridor to his office. He had barely sat down when there was a knock on the door and Constable Johnson came in. "Professor and Mrs Quentin, Sir," said Constable Johnson and withdrew quietly and as quickly as he could, having seen the expression on Professor Quentin's face.

"Well Inspector what have you got to say for yourself?" said Professor Quentin as he waved away the chair that the Inspector offered him.

"I'm sorry, Sir but we have found evidence that's puts Sarah at the scene of the crime and also in Jeremy's flat."

"Well there must be a reasonable explanation for this Harbury and we've come to take her home."

"I'm afraid that's not possible at the moment, Sir. I still have a few questions for her."

The conversation ran along the same lines for several minutes before the Quentins left defeated but with Inpsector Harbury's promise that he would keep them informed.

After being forced to encounter the shocked and indignant Professor Quentin, his usual jovial, mischievous manner nowhere to be seen and Mrs Quentin red eyed and silent beside him, the Inspector shut his door and hoped for a moment's peace but it was not to be.

There followed the disbelieving Dr Saunders whose shocked but practical manner had been much more preferable to young Patrick's anger and frustration at what he saw as this absurd development. The worst of it was that Inspector Harbury was troubled by the cause of action he had been forced to take. He was not a naïve man but spending the best part of the afternoon sitting opposite the stunned Sarah and having to look into those shell-shocked, disbelieving eyes had only served to increase the doubt that Inspector Harbury felt about the way the case was progressing and yet it was Sarah's earring that they had found in Jeremy's flat and Sarah's broach that Patrick had found by Jeremy Marchington's body. However, the shock on Sarah's face when she was faced with this had seemed so genuine. She had lost them. These things happen. Inspector Harbury's thoughts continued to run on as he tried to make some sense of the last few days.

Chapter 13

Constable Johnson's Breakfast

Constable Johnson was not best pleased. It wasn't that there was anything special about the police station canteen, it was just that since Mrs Johnson had decided to enforce a new healthy eating regime, it was rare treat to sit down to eggs, bacon and fried bread. It seemed that the time of death was by no means settled and so the Inspector had sent for Constable Johnson and insisted that he accompany him to interview everyone again. Constable Johnson's stomach did not feel at all settled as he thought of the eggs and bacon he had left behind in the canteen. He soon found himself at Professor and Mrs Quentin's house making notes as Inspector Harbury asked questions.

"I have the report back from the pathologist. There appears to be no doubt that Jeremy Marchington was poisoned." The Inspector paused to let his words sink in.

"Poisoned but none of us had even seen him, Inspector. How could anybody have poisoned him?"

"That, Mrs Quentin, is what we are hoping to find out. Where were you at around 5pm, Mrs Quentin, on the day Jeremy died?"

"I appreciate you have to ask everyone these questions,

Inspector, so I will try and remember."

"Thank you Mrs Quentin."

"I had a cup of tea with Charles and Sarah at about 4pm and then went upstairs for a lie down before getting ready for Eddie's party. I suppose at 5pm I was resting in my room."

"Professor Quentin?"

"As Patricia said we had tea and then she went upstairs to rest and I did some work on the paper I'm working on and then went to get ready for the party."

At this point there was a tap on the door and Rose entered.

"Sorry to disturb you, Sir." Rose addressed herself to Professor Quentin. "Inspector Harbury is wanted on the telephone".

The Inspector left the room.

"Harbury here. Yes, I'll be right over." The Inspector came back into the room.

"I'm sorry, Sir, Madam, but I've got some bad news for you. It's Dr Saunders. I'm afraid he's dead."

"What! But that's absurd." Mrs Quentin's voice shook.

"Eddie's never had a day's illness in his life."

"I'm sorry to say that appears to have held true to the last," Inspector Harbury's voice was grave. "The Constable at the Hall tells me that it looks very much like murder. If you'll excuse me Sir, Madam, I have to go and under the present circumstances I think Miss Quentin would be better off at home."

Chapter 14

It is Only Polite to Knock

Having entered the Hall, Inspector Harbury was greeted by the duty Constable and taken to the study.

"Morning, Tommy. I didn't expect to see you again so soon."

"I couldn't believe it when I got the call. I don't know what is happening to quiet old Hisbury. Absolutely shocking."

"What have you got for us?" The Inspector walked over to where Dr Fenwick was bent over the slouched body of Dr Saunders. He had been sitting at his desk and there was all too much evidence of the blow to the head that had made him fall forward onto the papers he had been working on.

"Well, all the signs show he has been dead under an hour. I'll send it off for analysis but it appears that this stone paperweight was the weapon. Seems like a spur of the moment thing. Perhaps he was having a disagreement and it got out of hand and whoever did it grabbed the paperweight and hit him with it. He would have been killed instantly. I'll keep you updated."

The Inspector turned to the duty Constable. "Who rang the station?"

"It was Marie, Sir. She was in a bit of a state having found the body. She's in the library being looked after by Constable Johnson."

"Thank you, Constable. Perhaps I can speak with her now."

* * * * * * * * * * * * * * * * *

Inspector Harbury was a sharp man but he was also a compassionate one and appreciated that, although these things were a way of life for him, discovering a body was always a shock for a member of the public and Marie had already had a shock when she discovered Mr Marchington's body. As expected, Marie looked shaken and Inspector Harbury tried to put her at ease.

"I know this is difficult, Marie, but if you could just tell me in your own words what happened this morning."

"It was early. Around 7 o'clock. Dr Saunders usually comes down at about half past eight so I thought it was odd that he was already up and in his study. I asked him about breakfast and he said he would have it at his usual time and that he was not to be disturbed until then. I went upstairs to do the bedrooms. It took longer than usual as Dr Saunders had asked me to make up one of the guest bedrooms as we were expecting a visitor. I was busy with all this and then helping cook prepare breakfast and so I didn't think anything else of it until I went to tell Dr Saunders that breakfast was ready at 8.30 as usual and that's when I found him. He looked like he was sleeping at first but then I saw the paperweight and....oh dear.....it was so horrible." Marie sniffed into the handkerchief that the Inspector held out to her.

"I understand, Marie. I won't keep you much longer. Did Dr Saunders tell you who the visitor was that he was expecting or when he was expecting them to arrive?"

"No, Sir. He just wanted the room prepared."

"And you've no idea who it could have been?"

"No. I'm sorry, Sir. I've no idea."

"And Marie, could anyone have entered the house while you were upstairs or in the kitchen?"

"Well people would normally knock and I would let them in and nobody did that."

"Could a visitor have entered any other way without disturbing you?"

"Well, yes, I suppose so, Sir. No-one in the village locks their doors during the day but still people don't just usually come in. I mean they would knock. It's only polite."

"Yes, well thank you Marie. If you think of anything

else, you know where we are."

Chapter 15

What Kind of Man Was Eddie

"Constable," Inspector Harbury's voice rang out across the police station lobby.

"Yes, Sir," Constable Johnson's head appeared behind the screen of the front desk where he had been enjoying a cup of tea with the desk sergeant.

"Get me the telephone number for Dr Saunder's solicitor."

"Yes, Sir." Constable Johnson hurried off and Inspector Harbury was soon on the telephone to Messrs Horningsham, Horningsham and Myers of Lincolns Inn Fields.

"Good morning, Horningsham, Horningsham and Myers. How may I help you," a rather adenoidal voice greeted the Inspector.

"I would like to speak to Mr Horningsham Senior please."

"Whom may I say is calling?"

"Inspector Harbury."

"Oooh. I'll put you through."

There was a click and then a calm, dignified voice spoke in to the telephone. "Horningsham here. How can I help you?"

"Hello, Mr Horningsham. Inspector Harbury here in Hisbury. I'm afraid I have some bad news for you. One of your clients, Dr Edward Saunders, has been found dead at his home."

"Oh dear, most distressing. Heart attack I suppose, poor Eddie."

"Well actually, Sir, I'm afraid Dr Saunders was murdered."

"Good Lord." Mr Horningsham's composure was momentarily shaken. It occurred to the Inspector that murder would not be considered favourable at Horningsham, Horningsham and Myers. "I suppose I should have realised that the police do not investigate deaths that occur from natural causes."

"I wonder, Sir, if you could let me know the provisions of Dr Saunder's will?"

"Well, yes, Inspector, of course. I had it drawn up for him after his wife died. I have dealt with his legal affairs for many years and he was a close friend. If I remember correctly, there were several charitable bequests, a generous annuity for his housekeeper and a bequest to his sister-in-law. However, the residue which, I must say, is a sizable fortune, was left in its entirety to a Miss Sarah Quentin."

"Thank you Mr Horningsham." The Inspector paused. "Do you know why Miss Quentin was the primary legatee?"

"Eddie did not share his thoughts on that with me but I always assumed that he felt close to Sarah as her Godfather and that having watched her grow up and having no children of his own, he felt justified in leaving his estate this way. You must understand Inspector that he was not close to his sister-in-law and the legacy he left her satisfied the feeling of duty he had to her."

"Thank you, Mr Horningsham. Is there anything else you can tell us that could help us find out what happened?"

There was silence for several minutes, as presumably Mr Honingsham went over his acquaintance with Dr Saunders.

"I really do not think there is anything I can tell you that would help you, Inspector. The fact is that Dr Saunders had me recommended to him and came to me to draw up a will when he got married. We became friends over the years but I do not know of anything that would explain what has happened. You reach a certain age Inspector and life rarely surprises you but I must say that I find Eddie's death shocking in the extreme. I trust you will keep me informed of developments."

"I will, Sir and thank you for your time." Inspector Harbury rang off and shot a frustrated glace at Constable Johnson.

"Saunders left everything to Sarah."

"But Sarah was with us when Dr Saunder's was killed."

"Exactly but it seems he was not particularly close to the little family he had and he was Sarah's Godfather and had known her since she was a little girl. That's all very well Constable, but where do we go from here? The man has no family that we know of, seems to be on good terms with everyone and the one person who gains financially from his death was helping us with our enquiries when Dr Saunders was killed. Get onto it Johnson. I want to know everything about this man's past life, every job he had, every business dealing, every friend, every love affair. There has to be something. People just don't go around knocking their neighbours over the head for no reason. Now we'll go back and finish speaking to the Quentins and then you can start investigating."

* * * * * *

"I can't believe it Inspector, Eddie gone and like this." Patricia Quentin's face was drawn and she clasped her husband's hand tightly as he sat down beside her. "I just can't believe it."

"I know that this must be hard for you Mrs Quentin but you may be able to help us. You knew Dr Saunders for many years. Is there anything you can tell us about his past life that might help us to understand why someone would want to harm him?"

"But surely Inspector he must have disturbed an intruder. Surely this can't have been planned. Eddie was a wonderful man. He didn't have any enemies."

"I'm sorry Mrs Quentin but he was struck from behind. There is no doubt he had at least one enemy. I'm sorry to have to ask you this but what were you doing this afternoon?"

"That's alright, Inspector. Eddie was a very dear friend and we want to do everything we can to help, don't we Charles?"

"Of course but I don't think we can tell you anything Inspector. Patricia and I were at home all morning. I spent most of the morning in my study. I left it only twice, once to get a cup of tea and once to go for a stroll in the garden. Patricia was writing letters and resting. You have to understand, Inspector that Jeremy's death was a great shock especially in a little village like Hisbury and now Eddie. It's unbelievable."

"It can't believe be true, Inspector. What earthly reason

would anyone have to harm Eddie? I mean there was never anything. He was married to Marianne for 25 years. I don't know what else to say."

"Thank you Mrs Quentin." The Inspector paused and then said. "I wonder if I could speak to Gemma Haines briefly, just some routine questions."

"Of course Inspector I'll go and see if I can find her." Mrs Quentin left the room.

"Sit down Harbury," said the Professor in his usual vague way. "I'm glad to have Sarah home but at this price. It's unbelievable."

"I must admit I've been shocked at the events over the last few days. If you had told me last week I'd be investigating two murders in Hisbury I would never have believed you."

"You know Inspector I've never really thought about it but if I had I would have thought that if someone was murdered there would be events in their life that would give you some clue as to why but in this case.."

Before the Professor had a chance to continue these musings, the door opened and Gemma Haines came in.

"Patricia said you wanted to see me, Inspector," said Gemma. She seemed nervous and Inspector Harbury quickly tried to put her at ease.

"Yes just a few routine questions." The Inspector motioned towards a seat as Professor Quentin tactfully left the room, probably heading towards his study thought the Inspector, smiling to himself. Gemma sat down and Inspector Harbury sat on the sofa opposite her.

"I assume you've heard about Dr Saunders?"

"Yes Inspector and I think it's very sad. He was always very kind to me. He treated everybody the same whatever their social position and I liked that."

"Where were you this morning, Ms Haines?"

"I was here, Inspector. I had breakfast and then Mrs Quentin said she had some letters to write and went upstairs and I was reading in my room."

"And what were you doing on the day Jeremy died, Ms Haines, at around 5pm?"

"Again Inspector I was here resting and then getting ready before the party."

"We have evidence that Jeremy Marchington was poisoned." The Inspector paused to see how Ms Haines reacted. He was well rewarded. The look of shock on her face was clearly apparent.

"I don't understand, Inspector, we were all in the other room when Mr Marchington was found. How could someone have poisoned him?"

"It appears that the poison entered his system several hours before the party."

"I'm sorry Inspector but I don't know what else I can say to help you."

"Well thank you for your time Ms Haines.

Chapter 16

Amanda And Teddy

Inspector Harbury looked across at Amanda. Her composure was unfaltering. He wondered how much she could tell him if she wanted to or whether she really just knew nothing. "How well did you know Dr Saunders?"

Amanda studied the Inspector before answering. "I had know him a long time Inspector but I would not say we knew each other well. We moved in the same circles and had mutual acquaintances but I would not say we were particularly close."

"Do you know of anyone who would wish to harm him?"

"I can't help you there Inspector except to say that Eddie was a good man. I never knew anyone that didn't like him. He was married to Marianne for years and then, since she died, he has lived a quiet life, doing as he pleased but not bothering anyone. "

"What about when he was young?"

"He was 20 years older than me Inspector. I didn't know him when he was young. However, I have heard rumours. You know what the theatre is like Inspector. It seems there was another woman but then he met Marianne. Word has it that this other woman left suddenly but it's perfectly possible, in fact probable, that she left for a perfectly innocent reason, but people talk."

"And what exactly do people say?"

"It was probably nothing, Inspector but there was an actress on stage at the time and her and Eddie spent some time together before Marianne came on the scene. She left pretty suddenly and there was some talk but I never believed it - Eddie wasn't that kind of man."

"All the same, it may be all we have to go on. What did people say?"

"Well they said that the girl in question would never have left unless she had to. She was rumoured to have been offered a big picture deal. She would never have turned it down unless there was no choice but she was unmarried and well in those days things were different...but Inspector.."

"Just one more thing. Do you remember the girl's name?"

"I only knew her as Lily."

"Thank you." The Inspector paused and then continued with his routine questions. "What were you doing this morning Miss?"

"I was here at home, alone."

"We have discovered that Mr Marchington was poisoned. Do you have anything to say that may help us?"

"Poisoned! But he had only just arrived at the party. No-one had even seen him."

"Could you tell us what you were doing at around 5pm on the day of the party?"

"I was getting ready. Teddy was here. It only takes about an hour to get to Hisbury from London so we left about 6pm."

"And you went straight into the party?"

"Yes, Inspector. You can ask anyone. They all saw us pull up in the car."

"Thank you, Miss. I'll be in touch if we have any more questions."

Chapter 17

Inspector Harbury Takes Stock

"So Harbury it's a busy time for you. You didn't have anything to do with these murders did you? Getting tired of dealing with the village disagreements and petty squabbling and wanted something you could really get your teeth into?" The Judge chuckled as he sipped his whiskey.

Inspector Harbury smiled in spite of himself. "I could say the same about you, Sir. Retired from the bench. Bored with retirement."

The Judge almost choked on his drink. "Wouldn't that be a turn up. I know some people who would love to see my name dragged through the mud. All those years I've preached about justice."

Harbury looked suddenly glum. "The thing is, Sir, that Hisbury is quiet and that's the way I like it and to make matters worse not only is there a murderer on the loose in Hisbury but the lack of leads makes it just as possible for it to be you or I as anyone else."

"Now, now Harbury. This isn't the man I know. You'll get there. What have you got so far?"

"Well, nothing much on Jeremy. Seems to have led a hectic lifestyle, lots of female friends but never made a secret of the fact that he didn't want to settle down. Eddie, the only hint of possible scandal is a woman he was rumoured to be involved years ago before he met his wife and there was talk after she left the theatre suddenly. The idea seems to be that she may have been expecting a child but if so she or her child never turned up. I find it hard to believe that one of them were suddenly seized with a fit of rage after all these years and came and hit Dr Saunders on the head with a paperweight. On the contrary from everything I have heard about Eddie Saunders if someone had turned up saying he had a child he would have made provision for the mother and the child."

"I'm sure he would have. He was a decent man. I'm sure he had his moments when he was young but I have never known him to shirk his responsibilities."

"The question is where do we go from here?"

"You've just got to keep at it man. Sooner or later you'll find something. It might seem completely unconnected or insignificant but it will lead somewhere. Remember what you are always saying that everything, even the trivial things need to be explained before the case falls into place."

"You're right of course but keep your eyes and ears open for me won't you. I need all the help I can get!"

Chapter 18

A Visit To The Vicarage

Inspector Harbury walked through Hisbury towards the vicarage. He stood for a moment in front of the church. It was a typical English village. There was a school beside the church and a village green with a pond. Then the village pub and a cluster of pretty little houses across the road from the church. It was towards one of these houses that the Inspector walked now. There was an old fashioned knocker on the door which the Inspector put to good use and the door was quickly opened by Julia Woodgrove.

"Hello, Mrs Woodgrove. I wonder if you and the Reverend Hcould spare a moment."

"Of course, Inspector. I suppose you'll be wanting to talk about Dr Saunders. I couldn't believe it when I heard. What an awful thing to happen. He and his late wife were such lovely people. Well I suppose he will be with her now."

"I suppose so," said the Inspector who, not being particularly religious, was not sure what to say to this. He paused politely and then carried on. "How did you find out about Dr Saunders' death out of interest?"

"Now Inspector you've been in Hisbury for long enough to know that news travels fast in a little village. I found out from Elsie in the post office when I went out to post some letters and she found out from George when he came back from delivering the post. Now would you like a cup of coffee, Inspector?"

"Not for me thank you Mrs Woodgrove."

"Let me go and find Raif and then you can ask us your questions." She hesitated. "Inspector I'm sure you've got a lot to do at the moment but you haven't got any news on my letters have you?"

"Nothing yet Ma'am. Forensics did have a look at them but they found nothing. I'll let you know if anything else comes to light and in the meantime if you get any more, you should let me have them."

"Of course." Mrs Woodgrove looked a bit confused and then hurried off to find the Reverend.

They were soon both sitting with the Inspector looking at him expectantly.

"Julia told me you have heard about Dr Saunders?" The Inspector addressed the Reverend.

"Yes such a terrible tragedy. I suppose an intruder must have got in?"

The Inspector almost felt guilty answering the Reverend. He was such a good person. Violence didn't seem to have a place in his ordered world.

"I'm afraid, Sir that Dr Saunders was hit from behind and unfortunately all the signs point to it being a deliberate murder."

"Good Lord, two murders, here in Hisbury!" The Reverend was clearly shaken.

"I'm sorry to have to ask you this Reverend but we have to get an idea of people's movements this morning and the afternoon of Jeremy Marchington's murder. Mr Marchington was poisoned and we have reason to believe he was killed several hours before the party at around 5pm."

"Of course, Inspector." The Reverend pulled himself together and continued. "Well, Friday's is my day for visiting parishioners so on the day of the party I was doing that from after lunch until about 2 o'clock until about 5 o'clock when I came back here."

"Yes Raif came back at 5pm and we had a cup of tea together."

"And before that Mrs Woodgrove?"

"I had a meeting of the Village in Bloom Committee from 3 o'clock which went on until almost 5 o'clock when I returned home. We had tea and then we got ready for the party and went over to the Hall."

"And this morning?"

"I was in my study working on my sermon and Julia was doing some gardening I think."

"Reverend, do you know anything that could help us? Anything at all?"

"Of course, I've known Dr Saunders for many years but only since he came to live in Hisbury with Marianne. I know he was part of the theatrical crowd when he was younger but I have never heard anything to his detriment. He was always an upstanding member of the community and very generous to the church fund."

The Inspector took his leave and left with the strong impression that anyone adding to the church fund would be ok as far as the Reverend was concerned.

Chapter 19

Inspector Harbury Has Visitors

Inspector Harbury sat down at his desk and glanced at the ever increasing pile of paperwork in front of him. I suppose I should make a start, he thought. There doesn't seem to be anything else I can do on the Saunders case until the reports start coming in and they will come in. He took down the first file and the pile tottered dangerously. He started to read absent mindedly.

Still I don't hold out much hope for anything useful, thought Harbury despondently. There just doesn't seem to be anything of interest in this man's life. I mean he had maybe one liaison before meeting his wife that might have resulted in a child that might have been his but just as easily could have been someone else's or most likely the girl got a better offer and went off to live her life. And even if there was a girl we have no idea who she is anyway.

Then he was married for 25 years and seems to be well liked by everyone. He seems to have led a very comfortable, quiet life. When Marianne died he was sad but he got on and enjoyed his life. He had friends whom he liked and who liked him. They spent time together occasionally in London for a show or dinner but more often down at the Hall. His daily routine in Hisbury rarely varied until one day when someone decided to wonder in and hit him on the head. Inspector Harbury sighed in frustration and pushed the file away from him. The huge tower of paperwork tottered precariously for the last time and finally fell to the floor with a crash. There was a knock on the door.

"Come in." Inspector Harbury looked up, glad of the interruption but trying to look serious and busy as if being disturbed was a great inconvenience to someone of his importance.

Constable Johnson's head appeared round the door. "Sorry, Sir, but I thought you would want to know?"

"What is it, Constable?" said Inspector Harbury.

"It's Marie at the Hall, Sir. She wants to see you. She's ever so worked up, Sir. I said you weren't to be disturbed but she wouldn't talk to anyone else. Insisted on seeing you, Sir."

"All right Constable I'll come now."

"Thank you, Sir. She's in interview room 1, Sir."

Inspector Harbury walked to the interview rooms. I wonder, he thought, I wonder.

He opened the door of interview room 1 and went in.

Marie sat facing him on the other side of the interview table. She looked tired and worried but then being involved in these things was difficult and she had found both bodies. The strain was beginning to show, thought Inspector Harbury.

Out loud he said, "You wanted to see me, Marie?"

"Yes, well, no, I don't know. I'm sorry, Inspector. It's just that this business has really got me into such a state. I can't sleep. I can't believe that this is happening. Hisbury is such a nice village and Dr Saunders was such a good man, everyone liked him. Who would do this?"

"Well that's what we are trying to find out Marie but as you say Dr Saunders was well liked. There does not seem to be anyone who would wish him harm but if there is anything you can tell us, anything at all that might help, I will listen. "

"Well, it's probably nothing and I forgot about it at the time. When I found the body it was all so awful that everything else went out of my head and anyway it was a woman and I don't think a women would do something like that. I mean it would be so horrible."

"A woman?"

"Yes I went upstairs to make up the guest bedroom as Dr Saunders had asked me to. It was when I came downstairs again that I heard voices coming from the sitting room."

"Did you recognise the voices?"

"Well, Sir, one was definitely Dr Saunders and the other voice I didn't recognise but I am sure it was a woman."

"Had you heard the woman's voice before?"

"No, at least not really, I mean it sounded like an older woman, sort of familiar but no I couldn't say I knew it. I don't suppose it helps much but I thought I should tell you. I mentioned it to Cook and she said I should come and see you. I got so worried about coming to the police station. I don't like being mixed up in this and I was worried I would be in trouble for not remembering it before but I only thought of it later. Cook said I would only stop worrying once I had told you. She said at least I would have done the right thing then."

"That's ok, Marie. There is no question of you being in trouble. You've been through a difficult time. Now that you've told me there's no need for you to worry and if you remember anything else come and see me."

"Thank you, Inspector."

Inspector Harbury showed Marie out just as Patrick was coming in. He looked at Marie with interest and she just glanced at him nervously and hurried off.

"Do you have a minute, Inspector?" said Patrick. "There's something I wanted to talk to you about."

"Of course, Mr Foley, come through to my office."

"I hope I'm not disturbing you too much."

"Not at all Mr Foley that is assuming you have not been entering any more crime scenes without my knowledge."

Patrick flushed at the memory of his antics in Jeremy's flat.

"I've been trying to keep out of trouble but there is something that has been playing on my mind. I feel I should tell you although I am sure that it has nothing to do with the murders. I mean Mrs Quentin is a highly respected member of the community and I wouldn't want Sarah to be upset. Really what I'm trying to say Inspector is that I think you should know about it but if it doesn't have nothing to do with what you're investigating then is it necessary for anyone to know?"

"Our job is not to upset people Mr Foley but we have a duty to find out what happened. However, if what you tell me doesn't have a bearing on the case I see no reason why anyone should know about it."

Patrick looked relieved. "Thank you Inspector. I knew you would understand."

"What is it that's concerning you, Mr Foley?"

"Well, it's something about the day Jeremy died. I was early for Eddie's do and I was strolling in the grounds. I've done that ever since I was a child, Sarah too. Eddie and Marianne never had any children of their own and they let us have the run of the gardens. There is so much garden that even when we played and made noise I don't think they could hear us at the house and even when they did, now looking back, I think they liked to hear children playing. Marianne often used to send Cookie out with little treats for us and homemade lemonade when it was hot. Anyway, so I was strolling around and then started heading up towards the house when I heard voices. I didn't mean to listen but before I had time to say anything it was obvious that the conversation was private and I didn't want to draw attention to myself as I didn't think they would have wanted me to hear and so I was stuck waiting for them to leave."

"Waiting for who to leave Mr Foley?"

"Mrs Quentin and Jeremy Marchington."

"Go on," said the Inspector trying to hide the excitement in his voice at this new development in the case.

"Well it was so strange. I know they have known each other for years but I didn't realise they were that close. They were speaking so seriously. I couldn't see Jeremy's face but his voice was strange, calm but angry too."

"And Mrs Quentin?" asked the Inspector.

"Well I could see her face as she was facing me and I had never seen her look like that. She looked upset and angry and terrified all at the same time."

"What did you hear them say, Mr Foley?"

"Well at first Jeremy said he was going to change his will but Mrs Quentin didn't seem very worried by this. It was only when he said that Eddie should be told that Mrs Quentin looked quite desperate and begged him not to say anything. I felt quite sorry for her really."

"Was that all?"

"Yes. Jeremy said he needed to think things over and walked away."

"And Mrs Quentin?"

"She looked upset and stood still for several moments and then she seemed to pull herself together and started walking towards the house. I waited a couple of minutes and then made my own way to the party and the rest you know."

"That is certainly an interesting story, Mr Foley. I appreciate you coming into see me."

"Not at all, Inspector. It wouldn't have felt right if I hadn't come but I am sure there must be a reasonable explanation."

"I'll look into it. Thank you Mr Foley."

The Inspector watched as Patrick walked away from the police station and reflected that at least there was something to investigate now but it wasn't going to be a pleasant task. He thought wistfully of the tower of paperwork in his office. This morning he would have given anything to have a lead that took him away from it but now he wasn't so sure.

Chapter 20

Marie Feels Better

After seeing Inspector Harbury, Marie felt a bit better. At least she'd done something rather than just worrying about it all and she was going out tonight so that would be nice.

I just hope things will go back to the way they used to be, thought Marie as she wondered along, thinking about her companion whom she would meet later. We could be so happy together if only we could get away. I suppose he's had a stressful time lately. It was all just so difficult. He's had such a rotten deal.

Life's so unfair and money is always such a problem, even with the extra I'm getting from Mrs Woodgrove for her cleaning and me helping her out with her other little problem, there never seems to be enough. I suppose he must be feeling the strain, thought Marie.

She walked back to the bus stop still going over and over everything in her mind. The worst thing is, she thought, I've still got to change all the bed linen before I can go out tonight and from then on her mind ran along purely domestic concerns as she paid for her bus ticket.

Chapter 21

Sarah Discovers a Secret

Sarah Quentin stepped out in to the sunshine and headed towards the Hall. She had been putting this off because the thought of going to the Hall and not seeing Uncle Eddie was too much for her but it had to be done. There was so much to sort out. She was very touched that Uncle Eddie had thought of her in his will. Of course he didn't have anyone else now Marianne was gone and they had no children but he didn't have to leave everything to her and he had. It wasn't the money, but she was touched to know how much he had thought of her. He had always been so kind and she loved the Hall so much. She had so many happy memories of it.

Sarah paused underneath a large oak tree and looked across the lawn towards the Hall, lost in thought. The sunshine, the smell of newly cut grass mixed with the fragrance of the flowers, the birds singing and the bees buzzing. It was hard to believe that anything bad had happened. Sarah closed her eyes and thought of all the games that she and Patrick used to play in the garden. It had been wonderful for hide and seek and they used to chase each other around until they could not run anymore and then throw themselves onto the grass panting and watch the clouds go by. And on those long summer days Uncle Eddie's cook, whom they had nicknamed Cookie, used to bring them home-made biscuits and lemonade. Sarah opened her eyes and looked at the huge trunk of the old oak tree. When she was little she could climb all the way round the tree and she could still see the footholds and handholds worn from so many little hands and feet climbing round and round. Sarah smiled. Uncle Eddie would always be remembered as long as the Hall and gardens were there. She was so glad she would be able to look after them.

She continued up to the Hall and saw that the front door was open and a bright red convertible was parked in the drive way.

"Brian Bartlett. Can I help you?"

Sarah started. For a moment the resemblance to Uncle Eddie was striking but as the man came nearer, Sarah saw that he was only her age and his hair was dark and wavy with no grey.

"Hello," said Sarah, recovering herself. "I'm Sarah Quentin. I just came to clear out some of Uncle Eddie's things."

"Pleased to meet you. My mother's first husband was Eddie's cousin so Mum asked me to come along and see if there was anything I could do to help. I was supposed to be visiting anyway and she is travelling or she would have come herself. I'll give you a hand clearing out if you like."

"Thank you. That would be very kind of you." Sarah smiled in spite of herself. Brian was so full of life and energy and it was nice to meet someone new in sleepy Hisbury. Sarah checked herself. She had to concentrate. After all there was so much to do. She followed Brain into the house.

"Well," said Brian, "where should we start?"

"Oh goodness, there's so much to do," Sarah sighed, suddenly feeling overwhelmed by the enormity of the task.

Brian looked around and then seemed to come to a decision. "Let's start upstairs with the clothes. We can sort through them and send some of the better things off to charity. Then at least you've made a start."

They made their way upstairs. Sarah felt very strange to be in Uncle Eddie's room sorting through such familiar things.

She glanced at Brian who was keeping up a steady stream of cheerful chatter
about his family and suddenly realised how glad she was that he was there. How could she have thought she could do this on her own. She said as much to Brian.

"It really is nice to have some help. This is not the sort of thing that would have been easy to do on my own."

"No problem," said Brian, "anytime. I have to go out later but I'm here for a few days so I'm happy to help. That's why mum sent me. I think she felt someone from the family should be here."

"Do you have a big family?" asked Sarah.

"No only Mum and me and my sister. Our father died when we were young so I feel responsible for mum and my sister who is five years younger than me. She's at school at the moment but she comes home for the holidays so I always try and be around then to see her."

They sorted through all the clothes and put them into bags for different charities.

"Well I've got to get going," said Brian. "Perhaps if you're free I could take you out for lunch one day?"

Sarah smiled. "That would be lovely Brian and thank you again for your help."

Sarah watched Brian turn out of the drive and then thought she would start sorting out some papers in Uncle Eddie's desk. But first I think I need a cup of tea, she thought and she headed off to the kitchen to see if Cookie was there. She found her just taking some rock cakes out of the oven.

"I heard you and Brian clearing out and I thought you could do with some refreshments," said Cookie.

"Oh thank you. I was just thinking I needed a cup of tea before starting on Uncle Eddie's papers. Will you have one with me? We haven't had a proper gossip for ages."

"Well why not!" said Cookie and she and Sarah settled themselves at the kitchen table with the teapot and a big plate of rock cakes between them.

"It's so nice to have you back in Hisbury, Sarah. Do you think you'll stay?"

"Well I'm supposed to be starting work at the solicitors in town in a few weeks but now I don't know. My heart was never in it and now I have this place to look after. I still can't believe that Uncle Eddie had any enemies. His life was always so peaceful."

"I know, a nicer man you could never meet. I've been very happy here."

"What do you mean 'been', this place would never be the same without you. You have to stay."

"Well it's very nice to hear you say that. And would I be right in thinking that there might be a family here one day. Mr Patrick is mighty fond of you and I noticed when Brian left just now he looked quite taken with you."

Sarah laughed and then suddenly looked serious. "But you know I don't feel as if I can think of the future until this awful business is cleared up."

"That's true. I can't believe something like this could happen in Hisbury."

Sarah nodded. "I just can't imagine anyone in Hisbury doing anything like this. I mean I grew up here and most people have lived here for years."

"Don't you dwell on it dear," said Cookie to Sarah. "Now do you want any help with your clearing out?"

"Thank you but I'll be alright."

Sarah wondered into Uncle Eddie's study and looked around at the book lined shelves and the comfy leather armchairs. She closed her eyes as the smell of smoke and cologne, leather and books hit her and she felt her eyes prick. She shook herself and moved quickly towards the desk and sat down. It had been kind of Cookie to offer to help her but she really felt she wanted to sort out Uncle Eddie's papers and personal things on her own. It was strange, sitting at his desk in a room he had loved, where he spent so much of his time but it made her feel close to him somehow.

Soon she was surrounded in papers. She quickly sorted everything in to piles. There was a pile of bills, one of personal letters, another of newspaper cuttings and a final one of people's calling cards.

She was just finishing and about to get up when she noticed another little drawer in centre of the desk. There was a keyhole but it didn't appear to be locked. It just seemed stiff. Sarah rattled it a little and it started to give, finally opening to reveal a pile of letters. Sarah recognised Marianne's handwriting and smiled to think that Eddie had kept them all these years. She picked them up, wondering what to do with them. It seemed wrong to throw them away although no one should read them. She put them on the pile of other letters and pushed the desk chair in disturbing Uncle Eddie's cat, Molly, who had been sleeping under the desk. Annoyed at being disturbed the cat jumped out from under the desk and startled Sarah who stepped back sending the pile of letters to the floor.

"Naughty Molly," said Sarah. "Look at the mess and just when I had got everything tidy."

Molly was pleased to see her childhood friend and she proceeded to walk in and out of Sarah legs causing her to over balance even more. Sarah laughed and stroked the cat's back and then bent down to pick up the letters which had scattered in all directions.

She started piling them up again into two piles this time and then something strange caught her eye. Why would mother be writing to Eddie she thought, we only live next door and she sees him all the time. Then she smiled. Oh my goodness I bet this was from years ago when she was in the theatre. Sarah picked up the letter thinking her mother would find it fun to see something from the old days and then her smile faded. It made no sense. Sarah forgot the mess on the floor and walked out of the terrace doors and started off across the garden. Her pace got quicker and quicker until she was running. All she could think about was getting to her mother so that she could explain this. She hadn't meant to read it but now she had…there must be some mistake. Sarah rushed up to the house and in through the conservatory doors to find Mrs Quentin sitting reading a magazine. She looked up as Sarah came rushing in.

"How the clearing out going?" she asked, "did you.." she stopped as she saw the look on Sarah's face. "Whatever's the matter darling?"

At that moment Professor Quentin came in behind Sarah. "Hello you two. What are you up to?" he paused taking in the tense atmosphere. "Is everything alright?"

"No Daddy it's not. I found a letter in Mummy's handwriting in Uncle Eddie's desk but its signed Lily. It says Uncle Eddie was my father." Sarah sank into a chair and covered her face.

Professor Quentin looked at his wife. Her white face and terrified eyes told him that it was true.

"I'm so sorry Charles but it didn't seem to matter at the time. Eddie didn't want to settle down and then I met you and I was so happy. You knew I was going to have a baby and you still wanted to marry me. You didn't want to know anything but I should have told you. I should have made you listen and then after we got married and Sarah was born, everything was perfect and I was terrified of ruining everything. Can you ever forgive me?"

Professor Quentin sat down beside his wife and took her hand. "There's nothing to forgive my dear. I said I didn't care about your past then and I still don't now. Eddie was happy with Marianne and we are happy together."

"You knew?" suddenly Professor and Mrs Quentin realised that Sarah was standing staring at them both. "You knew and you never told me."

Professor and Mrs Quentin looked at each other and then Professor Quentin got up and put his arm around Sarah.

"I'm sorry, Darling. Perhaps we should have told you. This is not the way either of us would have wanted you to find out but you have to understand that your mother and I love you so much and this does not change how we feel about you and how proud we are of you. Nothing could change that. And Eddie? He loved you so much and left the Hall to you not only because he was your father but because he was incredibly proud of the woman you had become."

"Oh Charles." Mrs Quentin hugged her husband and daughter.

Sarah suddenly broke away. "You have to tell the Inspector, Mummy. He needs to know. If only so he can stop looking for Lily."

"She's right Patricia," said Professor Quentin. "I will telephone him now."

*   *   *   *   *   *

Professor Quentin went out into the entrance hall and picked up the phone.

"Hello Professor Quentin here. Can I speak to Inspector Harbury please?"

"Yes, Sir. Just a moment and I will find him."

The Professor waited.

"Harbury here."

"Harbury. It's Professor Quentin. I wonder if you could come over. Something has happened that we think you should know about."

Inspector Harbury had the utmost respect for Professor Quentin and as such he agreed to come right away. Ringing off he called Constable Johnson and they set off.

* * * * *

Rose knocked on the door.

"Come in."

"Inspector Harbury is here to see you, Mrs Quentin."

"Thank you Rose. You can show him in."

"Good morning, Mrs Quentin. I hear you have something you want to tell us."

"Yes Inspector, I suppose I should have told you before but perhaps I did not have the courage." Mrs Quentin paused and looked at her husband who took her hand.

"It turns out Inspector that Lily was my wife's stage name before she met me. I always knew that Sarah was not my daughter by blood although I will always think of her as my little girl but her real father was Eddie Saunders."

The Inspector was silent for a minute trying to take in this new information.

"Well thank you for telling me this now, Mrs Quentin." The Inspector paused as if trying to find the right words. "There is also something else that has come to light that I need to ask you about, Mrs Quentin."

"Yes Inspector?" Mrs Quentin looked rather surprised as if after what they had just told the Inspector she could not imagine what else there could be.

"The conversation that you had with Jeremy Marchington on your way up to the Hall on the day he died was overheard. I wonder if you could explain to me what you were discussing."

Mrs Quentin blanched slightly and glanced at her husband but kept her composure.

"Well Inspector as I am sure you are already aware of the contents I will tell you what happened. Jeremy thought that Sarah was his daughter and that is why he left everything to me in his will. That day he told me he was changing his will. I had finally convinced him that Sarah was not his and that Eddie was her father. I was asking him not to tell my husband. I had also been to his flat on two occasions to beg him not to tell my husband or my daughter, once with a letter and once in person. I was a coward Inspector but I love my husband and daughter very much and I was terrified of tearing my family apart."

"And how far would you go to protect your family, Mrs Quentin?"

Professor Quentin stood up. "I don't like what you're implying, Inspector."

"It's alright, Charles. The Inspector is just doing his job and I never should have kept all this from him." She turned to the Inspector. "I have not always made good decisions in my life Inspector, but I am not a murderer."

The Inspector sighed and smiled at Mrs Quentin's determined face and the Professor's angry one. "I've known you both for a long time and I don't honestly believe that either of you would do this but frankly this case does not seem to be going anywhere."

Mrs Quentin smiled back. "Thank you, Inspector for coming to see us and I assure you that there is nothing else we can tell you."

After the Inspector had gone Professor Quentin sat back down. Sarah was sitting very quietly, looking out into the garden. "Are you alright, Sarah, my dear? Do you want to talk about it?"

"I'm alright. It's just a shock especially to find out the way I did."

"I'm so sorry, Darling." Mrs Quentin looked desperately at her husband.

Sarah saw the look. "It's alright Mummy. I know you would never do anything to deliberately hurt me. I can't pretend to really understand it but I'm not angry, really." Sarah gave Mrs Quentin a reassuring hug. "I just think I need a little time to myself to get used to the idea and get things clear in my head." And with that Sarah had gone up to her room and Professor and Mrs Quentin were left alone.

Mrs Quentin looked at her husband. "I'm so sorry Charles. You do believe me don't you. I never meant to hurt anyone. I was just so happy with you when we met and it seemed too good to be true that you didn't mind about the baby. I felt that was enough. I thought if it was a stranger who you had never met you would be fine but it would be different if it was someone you knew and then it just got harder when we moved here and Eddie was next door. I was so terrified of losing you. I was such a coward."

The Professor came and sat beside his wife and put his arm around her. "Perhaps you should have told me and I like to think that if you had then it would have made no difference but I'm glad you didn't because if there was even the slightest chance that my pride would have stopped me marrying you then my life wouldn't have been half as happy as it has been with you and Sarah."

"Oh Charles. I'm so lucky to have met you." Mrs Quentin lent into her husband and kissed him.

Chapter 22

Sarah Has Another Shock

Sarah felt better after a night's sleep. It had been a shock but Daddy, especially, had stayed so calm and he was right. They were a family and always would be. She wished she'd known sooner but she knew that Mummy and Daddy and Uncle Eddie would never deliberately have done anything to hurt her. It was Uncle Eddie's memorial service at the Church that afternoon and as she walked towards the Hall she felt closer to Uncle Eddie than ever before. The veranda doors were open so Sarah walked through them into the sitting room. She was thinking about other things and not really looking around properly but suddenly she realised that there was someone else in the room. She looked down, stiffened and stifled a scream. She walked over to the telephone and picked up the receiver.

"Inspector Harbury, please."

"Inspector, it's Sarah Quentin here. I am at the Hall in the living room and Marie is dead."

Sarah put down the receiver and sank into a chair. She could not believe it. It was like a nightmare.

"Sarah?"

Sarah jumped and turned. Patrick was framed in the doorway from the terrace in to the living room. Sarah sprang up and ran to him. "She's dead. I just walked in and she was lying there." And then as if knowing what Patrick's next question would be she added. "Inspector Harbury is on his way. I called him."

Patrick put his arm round her as his eyes fell on Marie.

*   *   *   *   *   *

"Hurry up, Constable and keep your eyes open. I'm beginning to think the Hall is not a very hospitable place."

Constable Johnson opened the car door for Inspector Harbury and shutting it after him they set off for the Hall. Harbury stared gravely out of the window.

"I can't believe it, Sir. Here in Hisbury. What is the world coming to?"

"I don't know Constable but Marie must have known something. She was dangerous to someone. We are still no nearer finding out who that person is."

"We know it was a woman, Sir. Marie heard a woman talking to Dr Saunders the day he died."

"Yes and she thought she recognised the voice and from what we've learned it could have been Mrs Quentin but she would have no reason to kill Marie now that Professor Quentin and Sarah know Eddie was Sarah's father which brings us to a dead end again."

By now the car had reached the Hall and as the front door was open, no doubt to admit the police surgeon earlier, Inspector Harbury and Constable Johnson walked in and made their way to the living room. Sure enough Dr Fenwick was bending over the body making his examination.

"Hello Tommy," Inspector Harbury greeted the police surgeon warmly, "I feel that I'm seeing rather too much of you lately."

"Yes, I've been called out too many times this week, especially for a quiet place like Hisbury."

"What happened?"

"Well it all looks quite straight forward. She's been strangled with her apron cord. Time of death I would say not more than two hours ago."

"So you would suggest a man is implicated or could a woman have done this?"

"Strangulation is usually a man's weapon, I would say, but I suppose a strong woman would have a chance especially if they surprised the victim."

"So, we're no further along?"

"Sorry Harry. I wish I could be of more help. If you finish at a reasonable time tonight, why don't you come to the Crown and I'll buy you a beer."

"Would love to Tommy, if I can get away."

Dr Fenwick left the room as Patrick entered.

"Sarah's having a cup of tea with Cookie. I thought she needed a sit down after this morning."

"That's fine, Mr Foley. Perhaps you could tell us what happened."

"Of course, Inspector. Well, I was having a morning stroll in the garden as I often do and I saw Sarah in the living room and came in. She ran to me and told me about Marie and that she had called you. Then I took her to the kitchen and sat with her until you arrived."

"And when you were in the garden this morning you didn't see anyone?"

"No, no one. Well, only Marie in the sitting room clearing up. Also Professor Quentin was taking a stroll and we said hello."

"Thank you, Mr Foley."

"No problem, Inspector. I'll wait out in the garden for Sarah. I think someone should walk her home once you've spoken to her."

"That's fine Mr Foley. I'll tell her."

*   *   *   *   *

Sarah sat in the kitchen having her tea. Cookie was bustling around as she had been for years, clearing things away, washing up and getting things tidy for whatever delicious thing she had planned next. It was all so familiar and comforting and yet everything was different. Sarah suddenly realised that Cookie was talking to her.

"Sorry, Cookie, I was just thinking how this kitchen is the same as when I was a little girl and yet everything has changed."

"Don't you worry," said Cookie patting Sarah's arm. "Everything will be all right."

"I suppose I had better go and see the Inspector. I'm sure he'll want to talk to me and you've probably got a lot to do."

"Don't you worry about that. Besides it's a quiet day today. There was no breakfast to do this morning as Brian is away and he isn't due back until later."

Just as she was finishing the Inspector walked in.

"Sorry to disturb you ladies but I wanted a word with Miss Quentin."

"I'll come now, Inspector. Shall we go into the living room if that's ok…?"

"Yes, everything has been removed Miss Quentin. We can talk in there. I will just have a quick word with Mrs James and then I'll join you."

"How can I help, Inspector?" said Cookie, fixing him with a steely glare that was quite unnerving.

"I need to ask everyone what they were doing at around midday, ma'am."

Mrs James sank into a chair. "It's wicked Sir that's what it is. She was a good girl. I mean a little silly sometimes, her head full of the pictures and young men but if you got her in the right mood, she worked hard. You had to watch her mind you. If you weren't careful she would get distracted and start dreaming rather than working and of course Dr Saunders let her go to the vicarage to clean on a Tuesday now so that was one day less for her to do her work here but generally she was coming along nicely."

"Can you tell me anything that could help me find out what had happened?"

Mrs James thought for a minute before answering. "You know Inspector she did seem excited lately. Come to think of it on the day of the party she was quite flustered. We were getting ready for the evening and there was plenty to do in the kitchen but she disappeared a couple of times and then came back with some whisky glasses from the dining room and ended up breaking one. Goodness knows what she was doing with them as the guests were going to be having cocktails but then these young girls need a lot of training and Marie didn't have a lot of common sense. She was easily led. And today again she disappeared and muttered something about clearing up when she was supposed to be helping me in the kitchen. That must have been when it happened. Poor dear and I don't know what clearing up she was talking about as Mr Bartlett was in London last night and isn't due back until later today."

"And do you know of any gentleman friends that Marie had? Did she talk about anyone in particular?"

"No, Inspector. She chatted away constantly and she was always thinking about young men. I had a feeling there might be a new one recently but no she didn't mention anyone by name. I'm sorry I can't be more help."

* * * * *

Sarah sat down on a chair as far away from the sofa as possible and she kept looking in the direction of where

Marie had been lying. The Inspector sat in one of the chairs and said in a gently encouraging voice.

"If you could just tell me in your own words what happened, Miss Quentin."

"I was coming up to the Hall to collect some clothes and things I sorted out yesterday to send to various charities. I suppose with everything that has been happening my mind was on other things and I wondered in from the terrace into the living room and didn't see Marie at first. Then I did and I knew she was dead. It was her face…so horrible. Anyway I called you and then Patrick appeared and I don't think I have ever been so pleased to see anyone."

"And then you went to the kitchen for a cup of tea?"

"Yes. Patrick insisted. He said it would make me feel better."

"He was right, Miss Quentin. You've had a nasty shock. I think that is all I need for now. Mr Foley said he would wait in the garden if you would like him to take you home."

"Thank you, Inspector."

Sarah went out of the double doors onto the terrace. Patrick was pacing up and down on the grass looking distracted when he saw Sarah and came over to her. She fell into his arms.

"Come on old thing. I'll take you home." Patrick put his arm around Sarah and led her across the lawn.

"Thank you Patrick. It just all seems like a terrible dream. I keep feeling that any minute I will wake up but I don't."

"I know darling but it's all over now. Everything is going to be alright." Patrick's voice caught and Sarah looked up at him. "You know how much I love you don't you Sarah?" said Patrick. "I would do anything for you."

Sarah squeezed his arm and they walked towards the house. Mrs Quentin was in the living room and jumped up at the sight of Sarah and Patrick.

"Whatever's the matter my dear? You look quite ill."

"It's Marie, Mrs Quentin. She's been killed. Sarah found her at the Hall."

"Oh you poor thing." Mrs Quentin led Sarah to a chair. "Patrick would you get the Professor please and ask Rose to make some strong tea."

"Of course." Patrick hurried off.

"It's alright Mummy really. Cookie already made me a cup of tea at the Hall. I just need to sit down that's all."

But Sarah's protest fell on deaf ears and for the next hour she was fussed over by Mrs Quentin and the Professor and Patrick until she managed to escape to her room for a quiet lie down.

*   *   *   *   *   *

When Mrs Quentin went to check on Sarah an hour later she was asleep but hearing the door to her room shut, Sarah stirred and looked at the clock. Goodness me she thought I must get up and ready. She thought sadly of Uncle Eddie as she got dressed to go to church for his memorial service. She had not gone to Jeremy's in London as she had not known him that well and with everything else going on, it had been difficult but she had to go to Uncle Eddie's to say a proper goodbye. She smiled fondly as she thought of him and once she was ready, she went downstairs to find Professor and Mrs Quentin ready in the hallway.

"I thought we would walk to the church if you feel up to it," said Professor Quentin as Sarah came down the stairs.

"That's fine, Daddy," said Sarah and they walked out onto the drive. Sarah took her father's arm and Mrs Quentin took Sarah's other arm and they headed off down the drive, out of the gates and along the road to the church.

When they entered, Sarah felt a lump in her throat as she saw the number of people that had come to pay their respects. Virtually the whole village was there and friends of Uncle Eddie's from London. Sarah saw Amanda and Teddy. Mr Horningsham, Uncle Eddie's solicitor, nodded at her as she walked up the aisle to find a seat. As she sat down she saw Brian sitting on the other side of the aisle. It was a very moving service and Sarah smiled to herself as she thought that Uncle Eddie would no doubt have approved of the service but would probably have joked that it would have been better if he was not the centre of attention. Uncle Eddie's favourite hymn was played and Sarah read a poem that she had written when she was younger that Uncle Eddie had always liked. After the service they all went back to the Quentins and there was a small spread of sandwiches and drinks and people chatted quietly before gradually going on their way.

Chapter 23

Harbury Gathers His Thoughts

"So Constable what do you make of it all?" The Inspector threw the case file on his desk in despair and looked expectantly at Constable Johnson.

"Well, Sir," Constable Johnston desperately tried to think of something to say that would justify his boss's faith in him. "I don't know, Sir." He finished rather pathetically and looked, if it was possible, more fed up than Inspector Harbury.

"You're right there, Constable."

"I am, Sir?" Constable Johnston desperately tried to think how he might be right.

"That's this case all over. We just don't know anything. Jeremy Marchington seemed to have been a man who was serious about his business affairs and relaxed about any other affairs but there is no evidence to suggest that anyone had a particular grudge against him. The only person who has admitted that Mr Marchington knew something about her is Mrs Quentin but once she told us she definitely had no reason to kill Marie unless she did poison Jeremy and Dr Saunders and Marie knew something but I doubt it. Everyone says Eddie was a wonderful person which isn't so unusual. We deal with exaggerated perceptions of people when they die but there really doesn't seem to be anything in his life to suggest otherwise. The only hint of scandal is this mention of Lily which I must admit brings us back to Mrs Quentin again and Mr Marchington was going to change his will so she would no longer have inherited but she doesn't need the money anyway…"

"You know, Sir, we do seem to keep coming back to Mrs Quentin."

"That's true Constable but it just doesn't fit. Something's wrong. I believed Mrs Quentin when she said she was terrified of tearing her family apart but I also believed her when she said she wasn't a murderer. If she is then she's a damned good actress."

"She used to be an actress, Sir."

"Yes but by all accounts not a very good one." Inspector Harbury paused and then got up. "Right Constable let's get it over with."

Constable Johnson nodded and they walked out to the car and drove off. The journey only took about half an hour and they were soon drawing up in front of a modest but neat little cottage where Marie's parents lived.

Constable Johnson got out of the car and Inspector Harbury followed him down the path to the front door. The Inspector knocked and the door was opened by a pleasant looking middle aged woman.

"Can I help you?"

"Mrs Jones?"

"Yes, Sir. What can I do for you?"

"My name's Inspector Harbury, Ma'am. I'm afraid I've got some bad news for you, about your daughter Marie."

Inspector Harbury broke the news to Mr and Mrs Jones. Mrs Jones was now sitting on the sofa crying quietly and her younger daughter, a pretty girl of, Inspector Harbury guessed about 20 years old, sat comforting her. Mr Jones's eyes had got a little brighter but his manner was aggressive.

"So do you know who did it then?"

"That's what we're trying to find out, Sir. I know this is a very difficult time but can you tell us anything that could help us? Did Marie have any particular friends we could talk to or any gentleman friends?"

"She didn't have any gentleman friends. Our Marie was a good girl, a little silly sometimes with her dreaming but a good girl."

Ten minutes later, having realised that that was all they were going to get out of Mr and Mrs Jones, Inspector Harbury signalled to Constable Johnson and they took their leave. As they were walking back down the drive, the young woman who had been comforting her mother caught them up.

"Excuse me, Sir but I thought you should have this," and she thrust a letter into the Inspector's hands. "It was Marie's last letter to me. She doesn't mention any name but she talks about a nice man. She was definitely excited but then she always was. I don't know if it will be any help but I thought you should have it."

"Thank you."

"You must find who did this, Sir. Marie didn't deserve this to happen to her. She was very silly sometimes but in many ways she was an innocent. She was so impressionable and she wouldn't have seen any danger."

Chapter 24

Quiet Old Hisbury

After everyone had left, Sarah had rested and then Patrick had offered to help her take the first lot of packages down to the post office. They walked in silence for a few minutes until Patrick stopped abruptly.

"Look Sarah about what I said earlier. I know this isn't a good time with everything that's happening but all of this has just brought it home to me how I feel about you and I just wanted you to know I am here whenever you need me."

"Thank you, Patrick. You are such a comfort but I don't think I can think about anything else at the moment."

"I know. I can't quite believe this is all happening in quiet old Hisbury. And Marie. Who would want to hurt her?"

"I don't know but I mean to find out. I know I've been known to complain that Hisbury is quiet and nothing ever happens but now…I wish that all this had never happened and things could go back to the way they were before."

* * * * * *

While Sarah and Patrick were lamenting about the state of events in Hisbury, Inspector Harbury was on his way to the vicarage to speak to Julia Woodgrove and the Reverend.

"Hello Mrs Woodgrove. Can I come in?"

"Of course, Inspector. What can I do for you?"

"It's about Marie at the Hall. I don't know if you've heard."

"Yes Inspector it doesn't take long for news to get around in Hisbury. Although I wish this had taken longer to reach me. I never thought I would see the day when this sort of thing would happen in Hisbury."

"I have to ask you and the Reverend what your movements were this morning."

"My brother is at the church if you want to catch him there. As for me I went into the village as I had a few errands to run."

"Did you see anyone?"

"I went to the bakers and brought a loaf of bread and then I got some stamps from the post office but apart from that…oh, I remember I saw Raif going into the church and I saw Patrick but I don't think he saw me."

"Thank you Mrs Woodgrove."

Chapter 25

Patrick In Two Places At Once?

Inspector Harbury knocked on the door and it was opened to him by Rose who had obviously been crying.

"Hello Rose. Can we have a word with you?"

"You'd better come in here, Sir" and Rose led the way to the living room. "It's awful, Sir. Who would do such a thing?"

"That's what we're trying to find out Rose and you might be able to help us."

"I don't think so, Sir. I mean I've been thinking and thinking but I can't remember anything Marie said that would help you. She always thought the best of everyone, Sir. I often told her to be careful, Sir. My mother always taught me to be wary of men, Sir. They can get a good girl into trouble is what she used to say. We weren't close, Sir, me and Marie, but she was so cheerful all the time you couldn't help liking her. You will catch whoever did this won't you, Sir?"

"We're doing everything we can, Miss," and then looking at the young girl in front of him he was suddenly angry at whoever it was who was doing this. Maybe Marchington and Saunders had a past but Marie. By God he would catch this monster.

Aloud he said. "So were you and Marie friends? Did you ever go out together?"

"Well we didn't really have much in common, Sir. She was always talking about the pictures and her film heroes and I suppose I'm more shy really, Sir. I like to read and go for walks but we were sort of thrown together both working in a small village like Hisbury so we did go out a couple of times, once to the cinema and once to the tea shop in town but we didn't always have the same day off so it didn't always work."

"And did she say anything that could help us to find out why she was killed."

Rose sniffed. "I'm sorry, Sir but it's so awful. She could be a bit silly sometimes Marie with her dreaming but didn't deserve what happened, Sir."

"Marie never mentioned any gentlemen friends to you?"

"No, Sir, at least."

"Yes," the Inspector tried to keep his voice calm even though he knew this could be important.

"Well she did say that she had met someone, Sir. She said he had big plans and that he was going to be successful and then they'd get married but she never mentioned a name. I didn't think much of it at the time,

Sir. It sounded like a line if you know what I mean. Poor Marie. Having said that she had been a bit flush with money lately. She brought me some tea and cakes when we went to the tea shop recently and she seemed to think that there would be more but then that was Marie. She would have believed anything and she wouldn't have seen any danger, Sir. She wasn't a bad person, Sir. She just only saw what was in it for her and not what anyone else might be thinking."

So there had been someone that Marie was close to. It could be important but then again it could just be some young man exaggerating his own ability to a young girl. Who hadn't done that in their time. The money angle was interesting though. That definitely opened up another line of inquiry.

As these thoughts were going through Inspector Harbury's mind, the door opened and Professor and Mrs Quentin came in.

"Thank you, Rose," said Inspector Harbury and Rose sniffed one more time and departed.

"Good morning, Inspector. You know this kind of thing is so trying for staff," said Mrs Quentin looking after Rose. "I wouldn't be surprised if she left us after everything that's happened."

"I wouldn't blame her, Ma'am. Hisbury is not a nice place to be in at the moment."

"Well let's get it over with, Inspector. I suppose you want to know what we were doing this morning?" said Professor Quentin.

"Yes Sir, and anything else you can think of that would help us."

"I don't think my movements are going to help you at all Inspector. I was walking in the hall garden. As a matter of fact I saw Patrick there."

"You saw Patrick in the Hall garden."

"Yes, Inspector. You know what Eddie was like about the grounds of the Hall. They are extensive and he was quite happy for people to take a stroll if they wanted to."

"Yes that's fine, Professor. It's just that we have evidence from another witness which puts Patrick in the village at this morning."

"Perhaps your other witness was mistaken, Inspector. I mean I actually stopped and spoke to him. It was just as I was on my way back home."

"And Mrs Quentin?"

"I was upstairs writing some letters and then I went down to the village to post them."

"And did you see anyone about?"

"I saw the vicar going towards the church on my way back from the post office but I didn't think that was unusual."

Inspector Harbury noted the tone of her voice and took his leave.
Walking back towards the car Inspector Harbury pondered on what he had heard this morning. Nothing very illuminating. Two different sightings of Patrick in two different places. Mrs Woodgrove says she saw him in town and Professor Quentin spoke to him in the Hall gardens. I must admit I would say the Professor was telling the truth especially as Patrick said he did go for a walk in the gardens this morning. Perhaps Julia was mistaken or, of course, she could be lying but why? She had a perfectly good alibi that he would check up on with the post office and the bakers. The trouble is he was back to that old policeman's nightmare that every witness's account of what they saw or didn't see was always so different and often very confused especially when it came to timings. But then it's up to me to work out who's lying, who's prone to exaggeration and who is just estimating the time, in short who is the most reliable, thought the Inspector with a sinking feeling.

Chapter 26

Sarah Does Some Sleuthing

The next day, Sarah went back up to the Hall to collect the rest of the packages.

The red car was in the drive again, which must mean Brian is here, thought Sarah.

She was just walking past the car when she saw a pair of feet sticking out of the bottom. "How was town?" Sarah addressed the feet which slid out to reveal a rather oil spattered Brian.

He grinned. "Not bad. Well better than this car anyway. Let's see if it's working now." Brian turned the engine on and after a bit of resistance it seemed fine. "That should do it. Well, since the car is fixed would you like to join me for spin? I could do with clearing my head. Maybe we can play amateur sleuths and get to the bottom of this business."

Sarah hesitated. "That would be lovely, Brian, but I have to get the rest of the charity parcels down to the post office and I'm not really dressed for going out."

"That's alright. Let me get cleaned up and then I'll run you home to get changed and we can drop the parcels off on the way. Come on. You can't expect me to explore on my own in a strange place."

"Alright. I suppose it would make a nice change after everything that's happened and you never know, we might come up with something between the two of us."

Half an hour later found Sarah and Brian pulling into the drive of Professor and Mrs Quentin's house. They were both in the sitting room when they went in and Sarah introduced Brian and went off to get changed. Coming down some 20 minutes later she heard talking and laughter coming from the sitting room and she went in to find Brian and her parents getting on famously.

Mrs Quentin looked up as Sarah came into the room. "Brian has been telling us he is taking you out, darling. I think it's a lovely idea and will take your mind off things."

"Yes we thought we might review the case a bit and see if we can come up with some ideas as to what happened. It seems so awful all of this happening in Hisbury where we know everyone. I feel as if we should try and clear it up."

"Whatever you end up talking about, it will be a nice break for you. Where are you going to go?"

"I thought we might take a run out towards the coast and perhaps even find somewhere nice for a bite to eat later," said Brian.

Brian and Sarah went out into the hallway as Patrick called hello through the garden doors.

"Hello Patrick," said Mrs Quentin. "I'm afraid you've just missed Sarah. Brian has taken her out for a drive. Such a lovely young man and it's nice for Sarah to take her mind of things."

"Yes, of course," Patrick tried to hide his disappointment. "Well perhaps I'll see her later then."

* * * * * *

Sarah and Brian had a lovely run up to the coast where Sarah went on holidays as a child. When they arrived Brian suggested a stroll through the town. They wandered along the high street looking in the shops.

"You know this place hasn't changed," said Sarah. At the end of the high street the road continued down to the beach where there was a little car park and from there you could walk onto the beach itself.

They walked in silence for a few moments just taking in the sea air and the view and then Sarah took a deep breath and said, "thank you so much Brian. This is just what I needed."

"It's lovely isn't it. You know I've always thought that one day I would come and live by the sea. Just walking in the sea air always makes me feel better, almost as if it washes any negative feelings away."

"Me too. Perhaps when I retire."

Brian laughed. "Listen to us we sound like an old middle aged couple."

Sarah blushed. "What about you Brian? I think you know everything there is to know about me."

"There's not much to tell. I grew up with my mum and my sister. As I said before she is 5 years younger than me so I've always felt protective towards her and mum. My father died when I was young and I suppose I've always felt as if it was my duty to look after mum and Brenda."

"It must have been hard for you though?"

"I suppose when I say it like that it sounds as if it should have been but it brought us closer together and I wouldn't change that and I think it's made me a better person. I couldn't really go out partying like my friends. I had to work and it taught me how important family is."

"I suppose I've only just learnt how important family is. I mean everything that has happened in the last few days has made me realise how I took my life for granted."

"It must have been a shock finding out about Eddie?"

"It was but Daddy especially was so amazing. He made me see that even though things weren't exactly how I thought they were, that he and Mummy and Eddie all loved me. Still I would always rather know the truth."

"In that case, to tell you the truth, after all this talking, I'm hungry."

Sarah laughed. "I saw a lovely looking restaurant just at the end of the high street. We might even get a table overlooking the sea."

"Right, lead the way."

Sarah and Brian walked back along the beach and went into the little restaurant. It was very quiet and the waiter rushed forward to find them a table.

Sarah chose a table in the corner next to a large bay window so they could look out at the sea. She sat down and Brian sat opposite her and picked up a menu.

"Umm I'm hungry," said Brian. "The sea air always gives me an appetite. I think I shall have the fish with new potatoes and a side salad and I will have a glass of house white."

"That sounds lovely. I'll have the same." Having taken their order, the waiter rushed off and Brian and Sarah sat back and relaxed.

"So, Brian what with everything that's been happening, I don't even know what job you do."

"I trained as a solicitor but at the moment I am taking some time off before going to work in London."

"Really? I studied law at university as well and I am supposed to start a job in London in a few weeks time."

"That's great but you don't sound very happy about it."

"I enjoyed my time at university and I loved studying law but I suppose it's strange to think that I have finished now and I actually have to start working 9-5 every day. Perhaps I just need to get used to the idea. I thought I needed a break but I haven't really had much of a rest since I've come home."

"If you could do anything, what would you do?" asked Brian.

"If I could do anything, I would be a writer," said Sarah. "Yes, I've always wanted to write although I thought I might write murder mysteries not experience them. The real thing is quite horrible."

"That's true. But you know if you want to write you should do it."

"I'm not sure what my parents would say about that."

Sarah and Brian continued chatting through their fish and then Sarah indulged in a chocolate cheesecake and then they both sat back to drink their coffee.

"Well this is lovely after the last few days," said Sarah when she was relaxing with her coffee.

"Yes I must say, I didn't expect Hisbury to be so lively," joked Brian.

Sarah laughed in spite of herself and then frowned. "It's awful though, I mean, I've lived in Hisbury my whole life and there are the little village dramas and you could never say that everyone always gets on but I cannot believe that someone I have known all my life could be capable of this."

"No. I mean I haven't been here long but from what I've seen of Hisbury I must admit I find it hard to believe that anyone could do this. It seems such a quiet little place and yet three people are dead. What about anyone outside Hisbury? I mean the party that Eddie had where the first man was found, what was his name?"

"Jeremy. Jeremy Marchington. Yes I suppose it must be connected with him as he was the first person killed and then perhaps Uncle Eddie and Marie knew something or saw something and the murderer got scared and killed them too."

"Umm," Brian sipped his coffee and sat back. He looked at Sarah. He had a twinkle in his eye but there was also a determination. "I think it's time you and I did a little sleuthing. After all I don't think either of us will be able to move on and think about the future until this is cleared up."

Sarah found herself blushing again and then said. "You're right about wanting to get everything cleared up. It is so horrible thinking there may be someone in Hisbury who is a murderer. But what can we do?"

Brian sat forward and assumed a business like air. "Well, we have to think about the motives for killing Jeremy and look into everything about his life. Was it money? Who benefits from his death? Was it revenge? Had he done something that had made someone hate him enough to kill him? Was it fear? Hisbury is a nice, respectable, English village. Did Jeremy know something that someone didn't want him to talk about? And then, are there any connections at all between Jeremy and Eddie? They were close friends for years. Did Eddie know what Jeremy knew or know about something in his life that would give someone a reason for murder? And Marie? Well that's more difficult. I think the most likely explanation is that she saw or overheard something that put her in danger."

Sarah sat up straighter, suddenly enthused by Brian's ideas and she looked more resolute. "You're right," she said. "We can do more than the police. People always hate being mixed up with the police but everybody knows me. I can chat to them and they will tell me things they wouldn't tell the police."

"Right! So we're agreed we're going to tackle this. I think we should keep it to ourselves though. We don't want anyone to get wind of what we're doing."

"You're right. We should keep it quiet and we definitely don't want to put the murderer on their guard but I think we can let Patrick in on it."

Brian agreed, although with less enthusiasm at the mention of Patrick, and they set off back to Hisbury.

* * * * * *

Sarah and Brian arrived back to the Hall to find Cookie waiting for them. "It's Mrs Woodgrove, Miss. She's in such a state. She wanted to see you and went to your house but they told her you had gone out with Brian so she came here. She's been here about half an hour and she wanted to wait. She's in the living room. Oh and the Inspector rang you Brian. He wanted to talk to your mother and said could you please call him back with her address and telephone number."

"Thank you, Cookie," said Sarah. "I'll go and see her now."

"I'll just ring back the Inspector, Sarah, and then I'll join you."

"Ok, Brian."

Brian went over to the telephone and dialled the number that Cookie had written down and left there.

"Could I speak to Inspector Harbury please."

"Harbury here."

"Inspector Harbury, it's Brian Bartlett. You telephoned earlier."

"Yes, Sir I wondered if you were free to talk. I wanted to ask you a couple of questions about Dr Saunders and I also thought your mother might be able to help me with some of the family background. She may know something about Dr Saunders' past life that could help us."

"Of course, Inspector. I could come over to the station first thing tomorrow morning if that's convenient."

"Thank you, Sir. I'll see you tomorrow."

*   *   *   *   *

Meanwhile Sarah had walked into the sitting room to see Julia Woodgrove pacing restlessly up and down with a distracted, worried expression on her face.

"Hello Julia," said Sarah. "Is everything all right?"

Julia Woodgrove jumped and turned round.

"Sarah. Thank goodness you're back. I've been so worried."

"Why don't we sit down and you can tell me all about it," said Sarah.

Julia perched on the edge of one of the chairs.

"So Julia," said Sarah, "what is it that's bothering you?"

Julia looked worried again and started rubbing her hands nervously as she talked.

"Well I haven't told anyone except the Inspector and of course Raif knows. He thought I was just being silly but they're so horrible and I can't think who's doing it and with everything that's being going on even Raif is worried now and I'm sure the Inspector thinks they are linked to the murders and I just don't know what to do. There must be a madman out there and I got another one this morning. I'm so scarred."

"What did you get another one of?" said Sarah.

"Horrible letters, saying awful things."

Sarah starred at Julia. "You mean poison pen letters, anonymous letters here in Hisbury."

Julia rummaged in her handbag as if taking this as a challenge. "I can show you. I have them here."

"Oh no I didn't mean I don't believe you. It's just incredible that on top of everything else someone is writing poison pen letters." She took the pile of letters that Julia held out to her. "When did they start?"

Before Julia could answer the door opened and Brian came in.

If it was possible Julia looked even more nervous.

"Oh, I'm sorry Julia," said Sarah. "I haven't introduced you. This is Brian. His mother knew Uncle Eddie. When she heard about Eddie, she asked Brian to come and see if he could do anything. Brian, this is Julia Woodgrove. Her brother is the Reverend here in Hisbury."

"Pleased to meet you, Mrs Woodgrove. I can leave you ladies alone if you prefer."

Brian could be very charming thought Sarah to herself and indeed Julia seemed to relax a little.

"No, no," Julia smiled at Brian. "If you're a friend of Sarah's then that's fine."

"Julia was telling me that she's been receiving anonymous letters."

"How horrid," said Brian. "When did they start?"

"March time. Before the murderers and my brother, Raif, thought it was just some silly prank and although it wasn't nice I didn't think much of it at first but then when Jeremy was killed I told the Inspector and showed him the last one I had received. What can he think except that I must be involved in everything in some way. You know what people say. There's no smoke without fire. If all this gets out people will think I must have done something to get these sorts of letters."

Sarah took Julia's hand. "You've lived in Hisbury for years Julia and no-one would think anything bad about you. Why don't you go home and have a nice cup of tea and a rest. You can leave these with me and I will have a look at them and come and see you tomorrow."

Julia's face relaxed a little. "Thank you Sarah," she said. "It's very kind of you. I know perhaps I shouldn't be so sensitive about it all but with everything else that has happened, three people killed now, I don't feel safe anymore."

Brian stood up. "Let me walk you home Mrs Woodgrove. I'll make sure you get home safely."

Julia smiled and took the arm that Brian offered as they walked out of the French doors. Sarah smiled to herself. Brian was certainly making friends fast!

Sarah sat down heavily on the sofa and sighed. She wondered if she and Brian were doing the right thing. There was obviously a crazy mind out there and they were going to try and find out who it was. She was not at all sure that she wanted to come face to face with the person who had committed the murders or written those letters. She looked down at the pile of letters on the sofa. They were neatly bound together with an elastic band. She couldn't imagine who would want to send these kind of letters to Julia Woodgrove or what an earth she might have done to make someone feel the need to send them.

* * * * *

Sarah picked up the letters and went out into the garden, closing the French doors behind her. She headed towards home. She felt tired after seeing Julia. The poor woman was so upset. Things like that shouldn't happen to people like her. She was the sort of person you always imagined in a little tea shop sipping tea and eating little cakes with a friend, probably gossiping about village affairs but nothing more. Surely she couldn't have something in her past that would cause someone to send these.

Entering the house, she went straight up to her room. It was a big room at the back of the house with a lovely view of the garden. It had been her room since she was a child although the nursery bars had been taken off the window years ago now and she had changed the wallpaper and added an armchair and a writing table. It was in the armchair she settled herself now. She took the elastic band off the letters and started to read. Half an hour later she laid the letters down and looked up with a grim expression. How horrible, she thought. No wonder Julia was upset.

Sarah got up and went downstairs to get a cup of tea. She felt shaken after what she had read. I'll get a cup of tea she said to herself, sort out a few things and then take these letters to Inspector Harbury. I definitely think he should have them all. You never know it may give him some clues as to who wrote them. Sarah had a few letters to write herself including one to the solicitors in town. She had decided to delay working for them for the moment. She was sure they would understand after everything that had happened. She went back up to her room and collected the things she needed and then went along to one of the spare bedrooms that also housed an old typewriter that was only used occasionally now. Sarah sat down and began to type. She finished the letter and took it out of the typewriter. Silly old machine she thought with affection as she looked at the letter "y" which had lost its tail. I suppose we should get a new one sometime and then she stopped and stared. She ran back to her room clutching her letter in her hand and picked up one of the anonymous letters sent to Julia. "It can't be," she whispered, "who would do such a thing? I mean only Mummy and Daddy and I and sometimes Gemma use that old thing. It couldn't be." Sarah made up her mind, picked up the anonymous letters and the letter she had just typed, then she walked quickly out of the house and was soon sitting opposite Inspector Harbury having just told him what she had discovered.

"So the letters that were sent to Julia were typed on a typewriter in your house."

"Yes, Inspector, but it doesn't make sense. It's only Mummy and Daddy and myself and Gemma who have access to that typewriter."

"What about anybody from outside? I mean could someone have entered the house without anyone knowing?"

"That's not a nice thought, Inspector but yes I suppose they could have. I mean, you know it's only a small village and people don't ordinarily lock their doors."

"Maybe until all of this unpleasantness is cleared up they should start." The Inspector stood up. "Thank you for coming and telling me this, Sarah. I will hold onto the letters for now and please be careful won't you?"

"Yes, Inspector. Thank you."

Sarah went home and was going to finish her letters when she heard the typewriter going. I wonder if that's Mummy she thought. Oh no she's out at that committee meeting and Daddy's gone to London. It must be Gemma. I'll go and see how long she's going to be and then take this letter to the post box anyway. Sarah went along the corridor and into the spare room. Gemma was sitting by the typewriter.

"Hello, Gemma," said Sarah cheerfully. "Catching up on some correspondence?"

Gemma jumped.

"Sorry I didn't mean to startle you," said Sarah.

"No that's okay, I was just concentrating. Actually I've just finished." Gemma got up hurriedly and the letters she had been working on fell to the floor. She tried to collect them up.

"Oh dear I think everything that has been happening has made me nervous," said Gemma.

Sarah came forward. "Let me," she said.

"No," Gemma almost shouted. "I mean it's fine. I can manage."

But Sarah had already picked up one of the letters and she starred at Gemma. Suddenly Gemma burst into tears and started sobbing. "I didn't mean to do it. I mean it was just a silly joke and then Mr Marchington was killed and the Inspector thought the letters were connected."

Sarah recovered herself. "But you can't mean that it was you. I don't understand. Why?"

Gemma sank down into the chair and tried to compose herself. "I can't tell you. You wouldn't understand. You've always had everything you wanted. You don't know what it's like to lose everything and have to take orders from someone all the time. Every little whim and wish, whatever time of day. Never asking how you are, what you are feeling. And your father always so patient and understanding and your mother not a word of thanks." Sarah winced at this slight on her mother. She knew she could be demanding but Gemma spoke with such bitterness in her voice.

"But why send letters to Julia? What's she got to do with it?"

"I thought if Julia received these letters she might think they were from Mrs Quentin. There was all of that business over the Village in Bloom contest. Julia wanted to run it and your mother had always done it in the past. I thought that she would be blamed and then maybe she would know what it was like for people to ignore you and not think you were something special all the time."

"You know that we'll have to tell Inspector Harbury about all of this?" said Sarah.

Gemma nodded miserably and Sarah felt sorry for her despite her disgust at what she had done. With an effort she got up and put her arm around her.

"Come on let's go and make a cup of tea and I will call Inspector Harbury."

Sarah and Gemma went downstairs into the kitchen. Sarah made some tea and settled Gemma down at the kitchen table.

"Here, drink this," she said. "I've put two sugars in and it will make you feel better. I will go and call Inspector Harbury."

"Thank you Sarah. You've been very kind."

Sarah went wearily into the hall and picked up the phone. "Hello Inspector Harbury please. Could you tell him it's Sarah Quentin."

There was a pause and then the Inspector's voice came onto the line. "Miss Quentin. What can I do for you?"

"Hello, Inspector. Actually I think you should come round to the house. I've got Gemma here and she has admitted to sending the letters."

Chapter 27

Exit Gemma Haines

"Constable, we need to pay a call on the Quentins." Constable Johnson and Inspector Harbury drove out to Professor and Mrs Quentin's house and the door was opened for them by Sarah.

"Hello Inspector. Thank you for coming so quickly. Gemma and I are just in the kitchen. She was very upset and I gave her a cup of tea to calm her down."

Minutes later Inspector Harbury was sitting in the kitchen opposite Gemma. She had said she was happy for Sarah to stay so Sarah and Constable Johnson had also sat down at the table.

"Now Ma'am perhaps you could tell us what all this is about."

"I'm so sorry. I know I shouldn't have done it and I was so scared when people started being killed but I couldn't help it." Gemma looked at Sarah pleadingly.

"Gemma has been telling me that it was because of my Mother, Inspector. She thought if Julia got letters like that people would think that Mummy had sent them because Julia had taken over the running of the village in bloom contest instead of her. Gemma thought if people thought Mummy had sent the letters they would ignore her and life would not be so easy for her."

"It sounds so horrid when you put it like that," Gemma said sadly.

"And what were you doing at around midday today, Ms. Haines?"

"You don't think? I mean I wrote the letters but I didn't kill anyone."

"We have to ask everyone."

"I..I went into the village to post some letters and oh dear I'm sorry.." Gemma began sobbing again.

* * * * *

Later that evening Sarah and Mrs Quentin sat in the sitting room. Inspector Harbury had gone and then Sarah had helped Gemma to pack and she had left to stay with her sister while she found another position. Sarah and Mrs Quentin had eaten dinner and were now quietly drinking coffee.

"Well, I still can't quite believe that Gemma would do that," said Mrs Quentin.

"I feel quite sorry for her though Mother don't you? I mean I don't think she was really a bad person. Life just went wrong for her."

"Don't give me that. Everyone has their difficulties in life. It's how you deal with them that counts. Besides I always knew there was something not quite right about her, I mean she was helpful and always did everything I asked but there was always something."

Sarah smiled at her mother's knowledge after the event and sipped her coffee. If only Mrs Quentin had the same kind of intuition about who the murderer was.

* * * * * *

The next morning, Brian drove round to the police station to see Inspector Harbury.

"I've written down my Mother's address and telephone number, Inspector and I telephoned her myself to let her know that you would like to see her. I don't know if she can help you. I know that she didn't see much of Eddie. Her first husband was Eddie's cousin and I know they were never that close although Eddie was always very kind."

Thank you, Sir. She may not be able to tell us anything but there is always a chance and in a case like this where there don't appear to be many leads, even the smallest thing can put us on the right track."

"You're right there, Inspector. I didn't know Eddie very well. I mean I'd only seen him a few times during my childhood but I can't imagine that he could have done anything to make someone want to kill him. All I can think is that maybe he saw something or knew something to do with Jeremy's death that made him a danger to the murderer."

"And when did you arrive in Hisbury, Sir."

"Well I arrived in Hisbury the day after Eddie died. I was working in London and Mum had telephoned me and told me about Eddie and she felt that someone from the family should be here so I came down. On the day Marie died again I had been up in town and then came back to find that Marie had been killed. I guess none of it is watertight but that's the way it was."

"Thank you, Sir." The Inspector paused. "You know I have the impression that you and Sarah and Patrick might be trying to look in to what's happened and make some sense of it. You will be careful, Sir, won't you? I would rather you left things to us but if you do come across anything, I expect you to bring it to me."

"Of course, Inspector. It's funny, at the beginning I never thought of it as dangerous but.." Brian paused. "You know you get to a point when you've started something and you can't turn back. You have no choice but to go on. I think that's how the murderer must feel you know, Inspector. I think he's getting desperate, either that or he's so cocksure of himself but either way at some point he will make a mistake and then we'll get him."

"I hope you're right, Sir. I really hope you're right."

Chapter 28

Harbury Has a Little Idea

That same morning Sarah had breakfast and then decided to pay a visit on Julia Woodgrove. She felt she should go sooner rather than later to break the news to her about the anonymous letters. She knew that Inspector Harbury had said he was going round to let Julia know that Gemma had confessed but Julia had been so upset that Sarah wanted to make sure she was alright. On the other hand she had felt sorry for Gemma and perhaps she wanted to give her side of the story to Julia as well. It had been a horrible thing to do and yet Gemma hadn't had an easy life. Reaching the vicarage, Sarah opened the gate and knocked on the door. She had seen the Reverend going into the church but hopefully Julia would still be in. Just as Sarah was thinking this, Julia opened the door.

"Hello Julia," said Sarah. "May I come in? I wanted to see if you were alright."

"Of course you can come in, my dear. I hear from the Inspector that I need to thank you. Come into the sitting room and you can tell me what happened. The Inspector gave me the bare facts but I really think men never really get the whole story. I would very much like to hear the details from you. Would you like some coffee?"

"That would be lovely, Julia. Thank you."

Julia made some coffee and set it down on the coffee table with a plate of biscuits.

"Help yourself."

Julia poured the coffee and then sat back on the sofa. "Now what on earth was all this about?"

"It wasn't really anything to do with you," explained Sarah. "Gemma was jealous of Mummy. She thought if she sent letters to you people would think they were from Mummy after you took over the organising of the Village in Bloom contest. She thought that if people thought Mummy was sending them, they would turn against her and not be so friendly. I'm so sorry Julia. I know it's been horrible for you but I did feel sorry for Gemma somehow. She should never have sent those letters but she was so upset. I don't think she was really a bad person, just lost her way a bit." Sarah paused. "Are you ok?" she asked Julia.

Julia started. "Yes I'm fine. You know I think I'm relieved more than anything. I was so worried about everything and scared. I've made my home in this village and have been very happy here. If everything had come out, I would have had to leave. At least now I know it wasn't anything to do with me. Just a misguided person who was probably very unhappy."

"I'm glad you feel like that and I'm glad I could help." Sarah paused. "What did you mean just now when you said if everything had come out?"

"Nothing, I mean…" Julia hesitated.

"You can tell me Julia. As long as it has nothing to do with the case then noone else needs to know."

"It was a long time ago before I met my husband. There was someone else. He was married. I was young and I had a child. There was no question of me keeping him, not in those days and so he was adopted."

"How awful Julia. You poor thing."

"It's alright my dear it was a long time ago and his adoptive parents would have given him a much better home than I could ever have done. He would be all grown up now and I'm sure I would be very proud of him. I often wished I could have told my husband but I don't think he would have understood. He was a good man but no he wouldn't have been able to cope with something like that. Thank you so much Sarah. That really is a weight off my mind." Julia smiled suddenly and then frowned. "There's still this other business though. I never thought I'd live to see the day when you couldn't look your neighbour in the eye without wondering if they have anything to do with murder. It's such a horrible feeling. You don't think it could be an outside person? Perhaps someone from London? That young man with Amanda seemed very shifty to me."

Sarah sipped her tea and thought that unfortunately the solution wouldn't be quite so easy.

    * * * * * *

Later that day Inspector Harbury and Constable Johnson sat opposite Mrs Bartlett, mother of Brian and his younger sister Brenda. Inspector Harbury had been quietly watching Mrs Bartlett ever since they had arrived. She had welcomed them into the house and been very pleasant. She told them that Eddie had been her first husband's cousin and they had never had much in common but Eddie had been very good to them especially since her first husband had died and even when she married again and had Brian and Brenda, Eddie had kept in touch and continued to help even when their father had left. She had felt that someone should go and see if anything needed doing and that's when she had sent Brian.

"Thank you for seeing us, Mrs Bartlett."

"That's alright Inspector. I know some people don't like to be mixed up with the police but I always say if you've done nothing wrong then you've got nothing to fret about."

"A very practical attitude. I wish everyone was as relaxed about talking to the police. Now, Mrs Bartlett, we really just wanted to find out anything you know about Dr Saunders. Did he have any enemies that you knew of or was there anyone who would feel bitter or angry towards him?"

"That's just it Inspector. I've been racking my brains ever since you telephoned and I just cannot think of anyone that would have had anything against poor Eddie. Of course he and his cousin were not that close, they were so different you see but we saw him every so often. If he was in this area, he would call and pop in, sometimes with Marianne. She was a lovely woman and that makes it all the harder you see because he was with Marianne for 25 years and they lived such a quiet existence. There was no scandal or gossip. They were just happy which is so unusual nowadays, don't you think?"

The Inspector nodded and waited for Mrs Bartlett to continue but she seemed to have paused.

"So there is nothing you think might help us?"

"I'm sorry, Inspector. I wish I could have been of more help. Eddie was a good man and he didn't deserve to have this happen to him. Not that anyone does. It's a wicked world, that's what I say. Would you like a biscuit, Inspector? I made them fresh this morning."

* * * * *

Inspector Harbury and Constable Johnson had eaten the homemade biscuits and then sometime later had managed to escape Mrs Bartlett's pronouncements on the state of the world today and were heading back towards Hisbury.

"The worst thing," said Inspector Harbury, "is that when someone is murdered all people seem to be able to tell you is what a nice person they were. It seems to me that unless we're dealing with a homicidal maniac that likes disposing of middle-aged gentry and maids then these people must have done something or seen something. There must be a reason for all this. We just have to find it."

* * * * *

Having gone back to the police station and absent mindedly rifled through some paperwork, Inspector Harbury decided to go back and speak to Julia Woodgrove again about her seeing Patrick in town when others had seen him in the Hall gardens. It seemed such a small thing but Inspector Harbury didn't like loose ends especially when three murders had already been committed.

He knocked on the door which unusually was opened by the Reverend.

"Oh hello, Inspector. I can't talk now. Julia told me you wanted to see me but I really have to rush out. It's old Mrs Hargreaves again. She's really suffering and she seems to find comfort from my visits."

"That's fine, Reverend. You go along and see Mrs Hargreaves. It's actually your sister I wanted to see again. Just a quick question."

"Fine, Inspector. Go on in." The Inspector went in and the Reverend got onto his bicycle and peddled off. The Inspector smiled to himself and quite out of the blue a picture appeared in his head of the Rev committing the murders. It amused him but somehow it just didn't fit.

"Inspector?" Julia looked out of the living room.

"I'm sorry to disturb you Mrs Woodgrove. May I come in?"

"Of course, Inspector."

She held the door open for the Inspector.

"Having a clear out Mrs Woodgrove?" said the Inspector seeing the old photos and papers on the coffee table.

"What? Oh no, not really. It's just with everything that's happened lately it makes you think about things."

"Yes, it hasn't been very pleasant."

"But you must be used to it, Inspector."

"Oh I don't know, Mrs Woodgrove. I think it becomes part of your job but you never become immune to these things and it seems to me that whenever I think I know human nature, it surprises me."

"Yes it's amazing what human beings will do for love or money or reputation. I sometimes think what I would do differently if I could go back." Mrs Woodgrove stared into the distance and seemed to forget the Inspector was there.

"Yes well I just had one think I wanted to ask you, Mrs Woodgrove."

"Of course. Sorry, Inspector. I've just got a lot on my mind. What was it you wanted to ask me?"

"It was something you said about seeing Patrick in the village on the morning of Marie's murder. It's just that I have another witness who has told me Patrick was in the Hall garden."

"Well they must be mistaken Inspector. I saw him in the village."

"Mrs Woodgrove my witness spoke to Patrick. Do you still think they could be mistaken?"

Julia had gone white but her composure was only momentarily shaken.

"Perhaps I was mistaken myself, Inspector. These things happen."

"You seemed quite sure just now, Mrs Woodgrove."

"Yes well I.." Mrs Woodgrove sighed. "I suppose it had to come out some time but please Inspector it has nothing to do with the case."

"Let me be the judge of that, Ma'am."

"I didn't see Patrick in the village that day."

"Then why did you say you did?"

"I didn't want him to be suspected. I had gone round to Mrs Quentin's to drop off some leaflets for the village in bloom competition. Mrs Quentin was going to hand them out at one of her committee meetings. Anyway I saw Patrick heading towards the Hall and I know he spends a lot of time in the gardens and I just didn't want him to be anywhere near where the murder had taken place. I know it was a stupid thing to do but I knew Patrick wouldn't do anything like that and I didn't want you to suspect him."

"I don't understand Mrs Woodgrove why would you…"

"Patrick is my son, Inspector."

Whatever it was Inspector Harbury has been expecting to hear, this was as far from what he could have imagined as it could possibly be.

"I told Sarah that I had a baby many years ago. It's funny you don't consciously think of something for so long and suddenly it comes up several times in one day. That's what made me get the photographs out, Inspector. It suddenly all came back to me."

Inspector Harbury still sat in silence.

"It was a long time ago, Inspector. I was young and terribly in love. Looking back though I don't think he felt the same way about me and after a while he disappeared and I never saw him again but I was expecting a baby. I went away and the baby was born. Raif knew. He helped me and then I met my husband. He was a good man but old fashioned. He would never have understood."

"And Patrick?"

"He doesn't know Inspector and I don't want him to. He's happy and the Judge has done his best for him. Of course the Judge knows it was me but I gave him up with the promise that his father's family would bring him up. The Judge was very nice about it. He understood. He knew his younger brother was always unreliable. You know the type Inspector, attractive to women but not steady. A few years after I was married, we got news that he had died in some far off place. It didn't surprise me." She paused. "It's funny Inspector. I used to be so scared of it all coming out but now telling Sarah and you is actually a relief."

The Inspector left Mrs Woodgrove's in a daze. Were there any more revelations in this small village that he thought he knew so well? Then frowning to himself he reflected that although he may have allowed Mrs Woodgrove to unburden himself, the fact that she had an illegitimate child over 20 years ago and felt the need to protect him from a murder he had no motive to commit didn't really advance the case.

* * * * *

Inspector Harbury went back to the police station to find Constable Johnson enjoying a cup of tea.

"Would you like one, Sir?"

"Thank you, Constable. I could do with one."

"Any developments?"

"Well, it's funny you should say that, Constable. I found out something quite substantial today that you would think would help us but doesn't appear to."

"Sir?"

"What would you say Constable if I told you that Julia Woodgrove is Patrick's real mother?"

"No!" The Inspector couldn't help feeling pleased at the Constable's reaction.

"Yes, it's true and it was such a little fib she told, trying to protect Patrick by saying she saw him in town when Professor Quentin spoke to him when they were both walking in the Hall gardens and then when I questioned her about it she broke down. Don't I always say to you Constable that every little piece of evidence is important and everything needs to be explained, however trivial."

"Yes but where does that leave us, Sir?"

"It leaves us Constable with a mother who will do anything to protect her child but as far as I can see we are no further forward."

"What I don't understand, Sir is why Mrs Woodgrove would say she saw Patrick in town and draw our attention to him when he might not have been anywhere near the Hall. It would have been different if she had seen him at the Hall herself."

"She was near the Hall that day. She said she dropped some village in bloom leaflets off at the Quentins. On second thoughts Constable perhaps you could check that for me. With so little to go on we need to make sure the little things add up."

"Yes, Sir, I'll get onto it right away." Constable Johnson went out returning some time later to find the Inspector still holding what must be by now be a very cold cup of tea.

"I spoke to the Quentins, Sir and at first they said yes they did get some leaflets dropped off but when I pressed them about the date it turns out it was the day after Marie's murder. Mrs Quentin was quite adamant because her committee meeting was the day after the murder and because of everything that had happened Rose had forgotten to give them to her and had just put them on the hallway table. Rose agreed it was definitely the day after the murder."

"Good work, Constable. That fits in with a little idea of mine."

Chapter 29

Plans Are Made

Sarah had arrived back from Julia's and had lunch and was in the living room when there was a knock on the door. Rose put her head round and said that Patrick was here and could he come in.

Sarah got up and went to the door.

"Hello, Patrick. I'm sorry I missed you yesterday. I was out with Brian. How are you?"

"Fine," Patrick smiled at Sarah. How he loved her! And sometimes he thought she felt the same way, but nothing could move forward with everything that was going on. Anyway he was going to rectify that. They were going to sort things out together.

"Actually I wanted to talk to you about everything that's been happening in Hisbury. I feel sort of restless as if none of us can really move forward until everything is cleared up."

"It's funny you should say that. Brian and I were saying the same thing yesterday afternoon."

"Of course but Brian can't know exactly how we feel. I mean we've lived here practically all our lives so it's so hard to think that one of our neighbours could do anything like this."

Sarah smiled to herself. Brian and Patrick were going to be difficult to manage.

"Anyway," Patrick was continuing, "I thought it's about time we did a bit of sleuthing of our own."

"That's exactly what Brian suggested yesterday."

"What did I suggest?" Brian tapped on the open French doors and wandered in.

"Oh hello, Brian. Patrick was just suggesting that we did some sleuthing of our own and I was just saying that's what we were talking about yesterday." Sarah got up. "Right! I'm going to get us some coffee and then before we get started I'm going to tell you what I found out yesterday afternoon."

Sarah went in search of Rose and coffee. When she returned, she settled herself on the sofa facing Patrick and Brian.

"Well," said Patrick. "What did you find out yesterday?"

"I found out that Gemma was the one sending the anonymous letters to Julia."

Patrick and Brian stared at her in disbelief. Brian recovered himself first.

"Gemma?" he said. "Your mother's companion? Why on earth would she do that?"

By this time Patrick had found his voice. "I agree with Brian. I don't understand why she would send those letters to Julia. What did she have against her?"

"It was quite sad actually. She wanted to get back at Mummy and she thought by sending the letters to Julia, Mummy would be suspected because they had a falling out over the village in bloom contest."

"But what did she have against your mother?"

"She was jealous of her. Gemma told me she had had a hard life and Mummy had everything handed to her on a plate and yet didn't seem to appreciate it and always ordered her around all the time. I mean she should never have sent the letters but I still felt sorry for her."

Sarah continued to tell Patrick and Brian about finding that the anonymous letters were typed on their typewriter and then coming back from telling Inspector Harbury to find Gemma actually typing one. Her audience was an appreciative one and Brian and Patrick forgot their differences as they listened with amazement to Sarah's story.

"I can't believe it," said Patrick when Sarah had finished. "You think you know someone!"

"Well I didn't know Gemma but from what you've told me about her she was the last person I would have suspected," said Brian.

"Well at least that's one less piece of the mystery we have to solve." said Sarah. "The question is what do we do next?"

"I've been thinking about that," said Patrick. I thought we should split up and talk to different people. I thought Sarah could talk to Amanda and Julia. It would be strange if Brian or I went but it would be quite natural for you to call on them and then bring the conversation round to the murders. The same with Cookie. She'll talk more to you than Brian or I. Then I thought I would speak to Teddy. Sarah and I can run up to town together and then if Teddy is with Amanda I can take him off for a drink. And then I thought Brian could speak to Professor and Mrs Quentin."

"That sounds good, Patrick," said Sarah and as she then turned to Brian and asked him what he thought he had to say yes.

"Right! That's decided," said Patrick. "How about I pick you tomorrow morning at 10 o'clock Sarah and we can have some lunch once we get to town before we call on Amanda?"

"All right Patrick. Wait though. We've forgotten your Uncle, Patrick. Someone should speak to him."

"True. I suppose I could," Patrick hesitated, clearly not relishing the idea.

"I think Brian would be better," said Sarah. "He could introduce himself and say he didn't know Eddie very well and your Uncle might speak more freely to a relative stranger than someone closer to home."

"Alright Brian it is then. Oh and also Rev Hargreaves. I can't imagine he will have anything to tell us but for completeness we should."

"Well you do that then, Patrick."

"No problem. I'll see you tomorrow then?"

"Alright see you then Patrick."

Patrick left and Brian stood awkwardly for a few moments.

"Well, I'd better be getting along too Sarah. I'll pop in later to see Professor and Mrs Quentin," and he went out of the doors and walked quickly across the lawn towards the Hall.

Sarah looked after him thinking it was so silly that Brian and Patrick didn't seem to like each other especially since they were so similar and for a moment when they were wrapped up in her story about Gemma they had forgotten all about how they felt about each other and actually got on well. Well maybe investigating this mystery together will be good for them thought Sarah.

Chapter 30

A Trip to Town

The next morning saw Sarah and Patrick speeding up to London. Sarah thought how nice it was to be finally doing something instead of just sitting around wondering about everything that had happened. She said as much to Patrick.

"You're right there. It's been hell just waiting for something to happen. At least now we can feel as if we're doing something. At the very worst it will keep us busy and you never know what we might find out. Not to mention that I get to spend some quality time with you. I thought I handled that quite nicely."

Sarah laughed. "It's nice to spend time with you as well Patrick but I do wish you and Brian would get along better. I think you would like him if you gave him a chance."

"Sorry Sarah - no can do. He's making a play for my girl!" joked Patrick and laughed.

Patrick was in good spirits and they had a lovely drive up to London. It seemed like old times again. They were soon driving through one of London's more prestigious areas looking for somewhere to park the car so they could have a lunch. Sarah had already telephoned Amanda and said she was going to be in London and would it be okay if she popped in to see her and had received an invitation to join Amanda for afternoon tea at 4 o'clock. Amanda had let slip that Teddy would be there so Patrick was going to tag along too and perhaps persuade Teddy to join him for a drink on the pretence of the ladies catching up. As they were in no hurry, Patrick suggested they have lunch at a small Italian restaurant that he knew. He parked the car and they walked to the restaurant and were soon installed in a quiet corner contemplating the menu.

"They do wonderful homemade tagliatelle here," said Patrick, "and you can choose from any of their sauces."

"Well in that case," said Sarah, "I shall have the salmon tagliatelle."

"And the tagliatelle with meatballs for me," said Patrick to the waiting waitress. "And a bottle of house white. Is that alright?" he asked, turning to Sarah.

"Sounds lovely."

They sat munching their pasta and exchanging university stories and Sarah found herself relaxing and really enjoying being away from Hisbury and everything that had happened recently.

After they had finished, Sarah left herself in Patrick's hands and he ordered them both tiramisu and coffee.

"Umm, that was amazing," said Sarah finishing her last mouthful of tiramisu. She sat back in her chair, sipped her coffee and smiled at Patrick.

"Thank you so much Patrick. That was really lovely."

"It was good but let's hope Amanda isn't hoping we'll bring large appetites for afternoon tea!" Patrick laughed.

"Well, I think I might have to go for a walk before heading to Amanda's. Since we're here I thought I might try and find a birthday present for Mummy. I so rarely come up to town and it would be nice to get her something special. What with everything that's been happening, I feel she could do with spoiling on her birthday."

"Well I've got nothing I need to do so consider me your chauffeur for the day," and with that Patrick paid and they left the restaurant.

As it was such a lovely day they decided to walk so, leaving the car where it was, they set off and spent a lovely hour looking in all the little boutique shops. Sarah brought her mother a beautiful silver bouquet of flowers broach for her birthday. While she was choosing Patrick had muttered something about running an errand and when he came back he was holding a little Chanel bag which he gave to Sarah.

"It's just a little something," said Patrick with a big smile.

Sarah opened the bag to find a lovely little bottle of Chanel No 5 perfume. "Oh, how lovely. Thank you Patrick but what's the occasion?"

"Nothing really," said Patrick, "just that it's nice to spend some time together. We should do it more often."

"I second that. You can take me out to lunch anytime." Sarah took Patrick's arm. "I suppose we had better head over to Amanda's."

Amanda lived in a beautiful apartment off one of London's well known squares. They parked the car and entered the building to be greeted by the concierge. As Sarah had visited Amanda several times before, they had no trouble passing the concierge and went up in the lift to the third floor.

Teddy answered the door and ushered them into the living room where Amanda was sitting with her feet up on the sofa resting.

"Hello darling," she said to Sarah and nodded to Patrick. "Teddy darling why don't you take Patrick downstairs for a drink and give Sarah and I some time to catch up."

As this was just what Patrick had been planning he acquiesced with enthusiasm and Amanda and Sarah were soon left alone drinking tea and eating sandwiches and cakes. Sarah thought to herself that she should not have worried about not having an appetite!

"So darling, what brings you here today?"

Sarah looked at Amanda and tried to decide on her plan of attack. "Well, it's everything that's been happening in Hisbury. Patrick offered to take me for lunch and I managed to do a bit of shopping. It's been nice to get away from everything for a few hours."

"And you thought you'd stop by and do some sleuthing as well," said Amanda archly.

Sarah laughed and marvelled anew at how shrewd Amanda could be. "Seriously though, not only can I not imagine who would do these things but I also can't understand what reason anyone would have to harm Jeremy or Eddie or Marie for that matter."

Amanda looked suddenly uncharacteristically serious. "You know you're right, Sarah. It's been bothering me too. I mean Jeremy was a good man. He wasn't the commitment type but he was always honest with everyone. It's just such a waste and I can't think why anyone would want to hurt him."

"Do you miss him?" Sarah asked taking advantage of Amanda confiding in her to ask this personal question.

"Yes I miss him very much. He's the only man I've ever really loved. I knew it could never come to anything. As I said he just didn't want to settle down. He never made any secret of the fact that he wasn't the commitment type and that was his choice but the world seems a darker place without him." She paused thoughtfully and then continued "and as for Eddie.."

"Now he really was a dear. I mean I know I didn't know him when he was younger but I can't imagine he did something that would make someone turn up after all these years to get their revenge."

"I agree with you. The only thing I could think off that is remotely connected with Eddie I told Inspector Harbury."

"What was that?"

Amanda hesitated.

"It's alright Amanda. I'm a grown woman now."

"Well there was some talk that a woman he was seen about with before he met Marianne might have been expecting a baby but I don't think he could have known. It may not even have been him and if it was and he had known he would have done his duty."

Sarah gave a half-hearted laugh.

"What's the matter, darling?" Amanda looked a little concerned.

"I'm sorry Amanda, but I'm so used to news travelling fast in a small place like Hisbury I forget it's not the same everywhere." She paused. "All the talk was true. The woman was my mother and I was the baby. Eddie was my real father."

"Good lord. Well I must say I am not often surprised but I didn't expect that."

Sarah laughed. "I must admit it was a bit of a shock to me as well."

They sat in silence for several minutes and then Amanda said. "Well in that case there really is no mystery in Eddie's past and as for Marie I think she must definitely have seen something that put her in danger."

While Sarah was sitting with Amanda, Teddy had taken Patrick down to the residents bar in the basement of the building and as was Patrick's intention the subject had turned to Jeremy Marchington.

"It's extraordinary," said Patrick. "I mean none of us had even seen him and he was just there dead in the hall. And the worst thing is the feeling that it might be one of us. I'm sure that's what the police think. What did you think of Jeremy?" Patrick took a drink and waited for Teddy to answer.

"I don't suppose it's any secret that there was no love lost between us. We were both interested in the same woman."

"I suppose now Amanda will need you more than ever."

"Perhaps." Teddy changed the subject and soon they were entrenched in a heated debate about the horseracing and then headed back upstairs. The conversation ran along purely social lines for a little longer and then Patrick and Sarah left to return to Hisbury where Patrick dropped Sarah off at the Hall to try and catch Cookie before she got busy preparing dinner.

* * * * * *

Sarah found Cookie in the kitchen as usual and they sat down with a cup of tea. "So what are you up to Sarah?" said Cookie who seemed to have an uncanny eye for getting at the truth.

"I suppose I'm just trying to find out as much as I can about everything that's happened and whether anyone saw or heard anything that could help explain things. I just can't believe it could be someone I know doing this."

"Well whoever it is dear, you be careful," said Cookie. "It could be dangerous."

"I suppose you're right. I hadn't really thought about it. I just wanted to get to the bottom of it all. I don't suppose you can remember anything that could help?"

"All I know dear is that Mr Marchington had a nice way with him and always treated everyone the same. It didn't matter who you were he would always say "Good Morning" or "Goodnight" and he always had a cheery word for everyone. As for dear Dr Saunders, I was awfully upset by it all. And Marie? She could be silly sometimes but she didn't deserve what happened to her. It really makes me angry that there should be such wickedness in the world."

Chapter 31

Brian Meets the Judge

Meanwhile, Brian had managed to get himself invited to tea with Professor and Mrs Quentin. This was mainly due to Mrs Quentin, whom he had succeeded in charming almost as soon as he met her. Brian was not conceited about his ability to charm people but he was a practical person who knew it was an asset in a case such as this. Professor Quentin, on the other hand, was much easier to manage, in fact he barely noticed who was invited for tea as long as Mrs Quentin was happy and he got his cup of tea and something to eat. As the Professor was working on an important paper he disappeared quite quickly into his study and then Brian did not find it hard to turn the conversation round to the murders.

Mrs Quentin said how awful it was and what a worry it had all been and then she looked at Brian. "I don't know how much Sarah has told you." Brian waited. "You should know Brian that I did make a mistake when I was younger and I was terrified that this mistake would tear my family apart but Charles has been so wonderful about everything and even Sarah has taken it in her stride. It must have been a great shock to her. I can't deny that it is a relief to get everything out into the open but I would never have hurt anyone."

Brian nodded in an understanding way but he soon realised that he didn't seem to be getting anything new from Mrs Quentin and after chatting for a bit longer he took his leave. Walking across the lawn towards the Hall, he met Professor Quentin who said he had come out of his study to get some fresh air, although Brian got the strong feeling that he was waiting for him.

"Mind if I join you?" said the Professor.

"Not at all," said Brian. "How's the paper coming?"

"Oh coming along," said the Professor in a unconvincing way. "You know all of this uncertainty makes it hard for a chap to concentrate. You start getting a bit paranoid and suspicious about people you have known for years."

"Yes, it must be very hard for people that have lived for a long time in Hisbury."

"Umm," said Professor Quentin in a even more distracted tone of voice than usual. "You know it's good of you to come to tea. Good for Patricia. She's been so worried about this especially her part in it. It's funny you know all these years I knew that Sarah wasn't my daughter and I knew there was a possibility Eddie was her real father but it really didn't make any difference." He looked at Brian. "I suppose that's hard to believe but when you love someone like I loved Patricia, nothing else matters. Can you understand that?"

Patrick looked like the Professor and thought how much Sarah was like him. Eddie might have been her real father but the Professor had brought her up. "I think I can understand," he said quietly.

The Professor looked at Brian with interest and then mumbled, "I'd better get back to work," and walked abruptly walked away back towards the house.

* * * * *

Brian started to wander back towards the Hall wondering how he was going to introduce himself to the Judge when he suddenly appeared walking in the Hall garden.

"Morning" he greeted Brian gruffly. "You must be Brian Bartlett? Patrick has mentioned you. Shame to make your acquaintance under such circumstances."

"Morning, Sir. I'm very pleased to meet you. Actually I was hoping to speak to you about Dr Saunders. I didn't know him very well but my mother's first husband was his cousin and she felt someone from the family should be here to help out."

"That's very good of her. Your mother's a good woman."

"You know her, Sir?"

"I used to, my boy. I used to. Her parents lived in the next village along from mine when we were growing up. I don't suppose she would remember me. She was a lovely girl. There was many a lad round here who lost their heart to her and I think she enjoyed the attention but then she met Eddie's cousin and that was it. There was never anyone else after that."

"I knew my grandparents came from this part of the world but I never knew mother grew up so close to Hisbury," said Brian.

"Well, she moved away when she married and made a life for herself and then met your father and once her parents were gone, I suppose she didn't feel much connection to Hisbury."

"What a small world."

"It certainly is. It's good to meet you Brian. Give my best regards to your Mother."

Brian watched the Judge walk away back towards his house and thought how you never really knew someone, especially people of a certain age who were settled and had been living in the same place for such a long time. It was easy to forget that they had been young and had their passions and heartbreaks and had made mistakes. He wondered what mistakes Eddie, Jeremy and Marie had made that had caught up with them so many years later.

Chapter 32

A Call from Inspector Harbury

After he had dropped Sarah off at the Hall, Patrick had decided to call on the Reverend although goodness knows what he was going to say. Luckily as Patrick parked the car he saw the Reverend going towards the church. Patrick got out and wandered in to the church to find the Reverend tidying up hymn books.

"Hello Reverend," said Patrick cheerily.

"Hello Patrick. How are you?"

"Good, good although very shocked by everything that's been happening in Hisbury these last few days."

"Aren't we all? I have been the Reverend here for many years and where there are human beings there is always some disharmony but murder? It is unthinkable."

"What do you think is behind it Reverend? I mean I've known most of these people all my life and to think that one of them had a secret big enough to murder for is unbelievable."

"I know and you know I feel like I've failed in some way. One of my parishioners has been driven to commit the gravest sin there is and has been pushed that far and not felt they could come to me for guidance to help them through the darkness and make sure they come out the other side without committing these atrocities."

"Yes well you mustn't blame yourself Reverend Anyway I should be going." Patrick beat a hasty and rather relieved retreat and the Reverend once again busied himself with the hymn books.

* * * * * *

Sarah finished talking to Cookie and then thought she would pay a quick call on Julia. She wandered into the village and knocked on the door of the vicarage.

"Hello, Julia. Can I come in?"

"Of course Sarah. How are you?"

"Fine. Actually I wanted to talk to you. Patrick and Brian and I are trying to make some sense of what's been happening lately and we thought if we talked to everyone then somebody was bound to have seen something that would help us."

"I'm sorry Sarah but I hardly knew Jeremy and or course I knew Eddie but only since living here in Hisbury but he was very kind. He let Marie come to the vicarage for one day a week, on a Tuesday, to clean for us. It's so hard to get staff in a small place like Hisbury. We paid her a little but I am sure that he made it up for us and I was always very grateful to him."

"I didn't know Marie did some cleaning for you. Still, that was Uncle Eddie all over. He was a lovely man and never really wanted any recognition for it. It just came naturally to him."

"Yes he was a good man. I'm sorry I can't be of more help, my dear."

* * * * *

Sarah, Brian and Patrick had agreed to meet for a drink at the Hall that evening to compare notes but this was delayed by a call from Inspector Harbury.

"Hello Miss Quentin I wonder if you could come over to the Hall with Professor and Mrs Quentin this evening. Some new evidence has come to light and I would like to talk to everyone together."

"Of course. What time do you need me?"

"Eight o'clock would be fine."

"Alright, Inspector. we'll be there."

Chapter 33

Harbury Makes an Arrest

According to Inspector Harbury's instructions Sarah walked over to the Hall with Professor and Mrs Quentin for eight o'clock. They found Inspector Harbury in the living room with Patrick, the Judge, Brian, the Reverend and Julia Woodgrove.

"Thank you for coming." The Inspector motioned them towards the spare chairs and they all sat down.

"What is this about Harbury?" the Professor voiced everyone's thoughts.

Inspector Harbury looked around at the assembled company. "This case looked so simple at first. Jeremy Marchington was killed and then Dr Saunders and Marie were killed. It followed that Dr Saunders and Marie's death followed on from Jeremy's, that they saw something concerned with Jeremy's death that made them a danger to the murderer or in Marie's case perhaps she saw something to do with Dr Saunder's death that made her a danger to the murderer. However, something Mrs Woodgrove said started me thinking."

"Me?" Julia Woodgrove looked startled.

"Yes, Ma'am you said that you saw Patrick in the village on the morning of Marie's death but Professor Quentin said he saw him in the Hall gardens."

"Yes I did." Professor Quentin chimed in. "We chatted briefly on my way home."

"Now Mrs Woodgrove may have been mistaken. She has told me that in fact she didn't see Patrick in the village on that day and that she actually saw him in the Hall gardens when she was taking some Village in Bloom leaflets to the Quentins. Mrs Woodgrove told me that the reason she lied was that she wanted to protect Patrick."

"Why on earth…" Patrick was incredulous.

"Why indeed, Mr Foley."

"No it can't be," Sarah was staring at Mrs Woodgrove who was looking at her pleadingly. "It was Patrick. He was the baby you gave up and that's why you lied to protect him. But Patrick didn't kill Marie."

"That's where you're wrong, Miss Quentin. I put it to you that Marie had found out that Julie Woodgrove was Patrick's mother. She cleaned at the vicarage and I think she found the old photographs and recognised them as photos of Patrick and Sarah as children that she had seen at the Hall. I think Patrick was terrified of people finding out that he was illegitimate and I think that Marie pushed him too far and he cracked."

"No." Patrick's voice rang out. "I didn't kill Marie. That's ridiculous."

"Of course you didn't Patrick." Sarah walked over to Patrick and took his arm.

"I'm sorry, Sir but you'd better come with me." Constable Johnson moved forward to lead Patrick out.

"It wasn't him. It was me." Julia suddenly jumped up and screamed out and then fell back into her chair and buried her face in her hands.

"I know it was you Mrs Woodgrove," said Inspector Harbury calmly. "However, it's nice to have confirmation."

Everyone starred at Inspector Harbury and then Patrick spoke. "You knew?"

"Yes, Sir. My apologies but the only way to bring this out in the open was to force your mother to confess when she thought you were being accused."

"I'm so sorry Patrick but I did it for you. It was as the Inspector said, Marie found out about you and she blackmailed me. I don't suppose she thought of it like that. She was a silly girl. I imagine she just thought it was a way of getting money. She wouldn't have realised the risk but I was running out of money to give her and I didn't want you to find out. I didn't want your life to be ruined with the scandal of you being born out of wedlock. I saw you in the gardens when I went to the Hall to talk to Marie. I begged her not to tell anyone but she refused so I had no choice. I didn't want to do it. It was so horrible. Even now I can't get the look on her face out of my head but I didn't want Patrick to be suspected. If it hadn't been for the Professor."

"Not just the Professor, Mrs Woodgrove. You also told me that you saw Patrick in the garden when you were delivering some leaflets for the Village in Bloom contest on the morning of the murder but I checked at the Quentins' house and you didn't deliver the leaflets until the day after the murder and that got me thinking. Then hearing that Marie worked at the vicarage I thought she could have seen the photographs and I felt that you, much more than Patrick, would have been terrified of the scandal. From what I had learnt about Marie's character and hearing from Rose that she had money lately. It all fitted."

Constable Johnson came forward and this time led a crying Julia away and the Reverend followed close behind them.

Everyone sat there stunned until the Inspector broke the silence. "Thank you all for coming over at such short notice and again I'm sorry to put you through that Patrick but I needed Mrs Woodgrove to confess. Otherwise, even if we felt sure she killed Marie, we only had circumstantial evidence and she could just have said she got her days muddled up. We couldn't have proved anything."

Professor and Mrs Quentin got up and Mrs Quentin went out followed by the Professor. "Well done Harbury," said the Professor gruffly as he left.

"Thank you, Sir," said Inspector Harbury and then turning to Patrick, Brian and Sarah he said goodnight and left followed closely by the Judge.

By now it was late and Sarah, Patrick and Brian sat silently not knowing what to say. Brian and Sarah also felt a little uncomfortable with Patrick after the revelation about his mother. Sarah spoke first.

"Are you alright, Patrick?"

"What? Oh, yes I think so. It's a lot to take in. Let's talk about the interviews we did and what we found out like we had planned to this evening. I think I just need time to let everything sink in."

"Well, I'll go first," said Brian and then he looked at Sarah and seemed to hesitate.

"It's okay Brian," said Sarah guessing what he might be thinking. "It's all out in the open now and we have to look at everything."

"Well," said Brian. "We know that Professor Quentin knew he wasn't Sarah's real father but he also told me that he knew that Eddie could be the father but that it didn't matter because he loved Mrs Quentin so much and I must say I believe him."

"Well I'm glad about that. Of course I would never have suspected him but it's nice to hear someone else say so too. And Mummy?"

"She said she made a mistake and was terrified of the Inspector thinking it had something to do with the murders and scared that it would tear her family apart but that she would never have done anything to hurt Jeremy or Eddie and again I thought she was genuine. What about you Sarah? Any luck with Amanda?"

"Actually, she was surprisingly honest. Perhaps it was a relief for her to talk about things. She admitted that she loved Jeremy very much but that he was not the commitment type. On the other hand she said he was always very honest with everyone about it, so there would be no reason for anyone to be angry that he had given them false expectations or let them down. That was it really and then Patrick and Teddy came back from their drink."

"Yes," said Patrick. "Well, I spoke to Teddy. He's not very talkative but he definitely has a jealous streak and a bit of a temper I would say. If he had any inkling that Amanda loved Jeremy then his temper might have got the better of him. Still, even if that were the case I don't know why he would have killed Eddie unless Eddie saw something and had to be silenced."

Brian sighed. "We don't seem to be much further forward. What about Cookie, Sarah?"

"We had a good chat but nothing new really. I also spoke to Julia Woodgrove. She just said how kind Eddie was and that he allowed Marie to come to the Vicarage once a week to do some housework but nothing to help us. I suppose after what the Inspector discovered, could she have killed Jeremy and Eddie? But what motive would she have had?"

"The same with the Reverend," Patrick chipped in. "He was distressed that one of his parishioners had been troubled enough to commit murder but he didn't tell me anything new. Brian, what about my Uncle? Anything new there?"

"Oh goodness, I should have told you that one first. I don't really think it's got anything to do with the murders but he was sweet on my mother when she was growing up in the next village along from Hisbury."

Patrick laughed. "Goodness I can't imagine Uncle being sweet on anyone. He's such a confirmed old bachelor."

"I must admit it did come as quite a shock!" said Brian. "You don't really think of your parents being young and having these emotions! Still it doesn't really get us anywhere. Where do we go from here?"

"Well, I've got to head off. I think I need to talk a few things over with my Uncle." Patrick looked a little grim while he said this. "I'll see you both tomorrow."

"Alright. Good luck Patrick. Let us know if you need anything."

"Thanks, Sarah. I'll talk to you tomorrow." And with that Patrick strode off across the lawn.

"Would you like another drink?" Brian smiled at Sarah.

"Sorry? Oh yes please. Thank you, Brian."

"You seemed distracted. What are you thinking about?" said Brian as he poured the drinks.

"Oh nothing. There was just something Cookie said the other day that I meant to ask Patrick about. It's probably nothing but it was just a bit strange."

"What was it?"

"Well it was after Marie was killed and Cookie said that Marie seemed to think Patrick was keen on her and was always flattering her. Cookie said she knew Marie was just being silly and I'm sure she was but I was just going to mention it to Patrick since we're going over everything."

"You should ask him you know," said Brian, handing Sarah a drink. "I mean we don't know if Patrick has an alibi."

"What, Patrick? I've known him since I was a child."

Brian looked suddenly a little sullen. "Well I think we should suspect everyone."

Sarah was a fair minded person and although she agreed that they had to consider everything and everyone, she was suspicious of Brian's motives in encouraging her to suspect Patrick. She stood up and put her drink down. "I think it's time I headed home," she said.

"I'll walk with you," said Brian, getting up.

"No thank you," replied Sarah and she walked out of the terrace doors towards her parents' house.

"Damn," said Brian to himself as he watched Sarah walk away.

Chapter 34

The Judge Explains

Having left Sarah and Brian talking, Patrick walked across the lawn of the Hall towards home. Home. What a joke thought Patrick. The Hall, it's gardens, his Uncle's house, was all so familiar to him but now it seemed alien, as if he didn't really belong but then he'd never really belonged had he? I mean Uncle had always been very kind but there was always a question mark over where he came from, who his mother was, what happened to his father and had his Uncle even wanted him in the first place. Uncle had done his duty but he never married. I think he would have been happier if it had just been him thought Patrick bitterly. He opened the door of his Uncle's house and walked in determined to thrash things out once and for all. He marched across the hallway to his Uncle's study and knocked on the door.

"Yes?" the familiar voice rang out. "Hello Patrick, my boy. Have you had a good evening?"

"Julia Woodgrove was arrested for Marie's murder this evening at the Hall. She confessed."

"What?" The Judge looked shocked.

Patrick just stood staring at him. "Did you know she was my mother?"

"Oh my boy I.."

"Tell me the truth."

"Sit down, Patrick." Patrick stayed standing and the Judge continued. "I always knew you would have to know some day and perhaps I should have told you before but it was one of those impossible situations. It was a different world then."

"She did it for me you know. Marie had found out that she was my mother and was blackmailing her. She was afraid of the scandal, was afraid it would ruin my life. What she didn't know was that she and my father had already ruined my life. He disappeared and she gave me away."

"Patrick she loved you. She just didn't think she had a choice and perhaps she didn't in those days. Even now.." The Judge went quiet.

"And you? You only did your duty. I mean I don't really belong here."

"Yes I did my duty and yes I'm an old bachelor who would never have had children by choice but now that I've watched you grow up, I love you as you were my own son and I would not have changed the way things happened for the world."

Patrick sat down and the Judge leaned forward towards him. "You know Patrick it's not where you come from that counts, it's what you become. I've spent my life looking at people who have ruined their lives with crime and they come from all walks of life. Perhaps your family background isn't the way you would want it to be but you're a man now and you can build your own life and be whatever you want to be."

"I just wish I believed that," said Patrick sadly.

The Judge poured them both a drink.

Chapter 35

Love Is in the Air

Sarah woke up the next morning feeling out of sorts. It was just too much to deal with on top of everything else. Patrick and Brian were just being ridiculous. She got dressed and headed downstairs to find her parents just finishing breakfast.

"Morning, Darling," Mrs Quentin greeted her daughter.

"Morning," replied Sarah as Mrs Quentin hurried out, probably to one of her many committee meetings.

Professor Quentin drank his last bit of coffee and got up and headed towards his study, stopping to give his daughter a kiss on the cheek.

Sarah sat down and helped herself to bacon and eggs, toast and coffee and started eating. A good breakfast always made her feel better. She was just finishing when the phone rang. Sarah carried on sipping her coffee and then after a couple more rings she got up to answer it. Where is everyone? she thought as she picked up the receiver. "Hello, Hisbury 434."

"Morning, Sarah. Sorry to call so early but I've got a few errands to run and then I wondered if you wanted to come over for lunch. Uncle's out so we can have a good catch-up. What do you think? About half past twelve?"

Sarah smiled in spite of herself. Patrick always sounded so cheerful and full of life. She suddenly felt better. "That sounds nice. Thank you, Patrick. I'll see you then."

Just as she was putting the receiver down the doorbell rang. Goodness me, thought Sarah, it's like Piccadilly Circus here this morning. She went to open the door to what turned out to be a very apologetic Brian with a bunch of flowers.

"I just wanted to say I'm sorry about yesterday, Sarah."

"Well I suppose you had better come in for some coffee then," said Sarah with a twinkle in her eye as she smelt the flowers. "I'll ask Rose for some fresh coffee and put these in water. Why don't you go into the living room and make yourself comfortable."

Sarah went down to the kitchen. "Rose could Brian and I have some coffee, please."

"Of course, Miss. I'll bring it up. Would you like some of Martha's homemade cookies as well?"

"Always," said Sarah. "Thank you, Rose."

Having left Rose to make the coffee, Sarah found a vase and headed back up to the living room. She put the vase on the coffee table and started arranging the flowers. Brian watched as she deftly place flower after flower to create a very pretty and original arrangement. Sarah finished to find Brian still watching her.

"You look very serious," she said. "Are you thinking about the case?"

"No I was thinking that I would be glad when the case is over so I can tell you how I feel."

"Brian don't. I…"

"I'm sorry but I have to tell you. I know I behaved like an idiot yesterday because I was jealous of Patrick. I know you've known him all your life and if you tell me you want to be with him then I will never mention this again but I have to tell you that I am here if you ever want someone else. I would do anything to make you happy."

To her surprise Sarah felt an excitement and expectation at Brian's words that she had never felt before. She has always felt so comfortable with Patrick. They had known each other their whole lives and it was just assumed that one day they would be together but with Brian? Sarah suddenly realised that he had stopped speaking.

"Thank you Brian. That was a lovely thing to say but I just need time. It seems impossible to think about anything else except the case at the moment."

"I know and that's fine but I had to tell you how I felt and that's not going to change so when you do decide I will be here if you want me to be."

Sarah was saved from saying anything else by Mrs Quentin coming in from the garden.

"Brian, how lovely to see you."

"It's lovely to see you too, Mrs Quentin. I was actually going to see if Sarah wanted to join me for some lunch later."

"I'm so sorry Brian but Patrick rang me just before you arrived and asked me to lunch. Perhaps we could do something tomorrow."

"No problem. Well I should get going. Nice to see you, Sarah. Mrs Quentin."

"I really do like Brian, Sarah. I wonder if he will be staying much longer."

"I don't know mother. Perhaps you should ask him," said Sarah archly as she went out of the room.

Chapter 36

Brian Makes A Decision

Walking away from the Quentins, Brian's thoughts were very confused. It was strange to think that he had only arrived in Hisbury a matter of days ago and his life had changed beyond all recognition. He knew Sarah was the one, the person he was meant to spend his life with but what he didn't know was how she felt. It felt so right and yet Sarah had known Patrick her whole life. How could he compete with that? He pushed these thoughts to the back of his mind and tried to concentrate on the case. After all he was a practical person and he knew that no-one could move forward until the murderer was caught. He knew what he had to do. The problem was what would Sarah think of him for doing it. Brian paused and then walked purposefully back to the Hall, got in his car and drove the few miles to the police station. He parked the car and walked in and addressed the Constable behind the front desk.

"Is Inspector Harbury in?"

"I can find out for you, Sir. Can I take your name?"

"Brian Bartlett."

"If you'll just wait a moment, I'll try and find him."

The Constable picked up the phone. "Constable Johnson. Is the Inspector around? There is a Brian Bartlett here to see him."

"Alright. I'll let him know."

"Somebody will be right down, Sir."

Brian paced up and down in the reception of the police station until the double doors opened and Inspector Harbury came forward to greet him.

"Mr Bartlett, what can I do for you?"

"I've got something very important I need to talk to you about, Inspector."

Chapter 37

The Judge Pays a Visit

As Brian left the Quentins, the Judge was heading towards the house to see Professor Quentin. They didn't often call on each other but both being academics and having a similar view of the world, they had an understanding and over the years had become good friends.

"Hello, Rose," said the Judge as Rose answered the door to him. "Is Professor Quentin in?"

"Yes, Sir. He's in his study. Shall I tell him you're here?"

"No that's fine, thanks. I'll just go and knock. Thank you, my dear."

The Judge crossed the hallway and knocked on the study door.

"Come," was Professor Quentin's rather abrupt greeting.

"Hello, Charles. Are you alright to have a break?"

"For you old boy of course. Would you like a coffee?"

"Thank you."

Professor Quentin went off in search of coffee and soon they were both sitting opposite each other in the two leather chairs in front of the fireplace in the Professor's study. Sitting where he had often sat before calmed the Judge and he began to feel better.

"I thought I might see you this morning," said Professor Quentin, who knew his old friend well. "Did young Patrick kick up a fuss last night?"

"It wasn't as bad as I would have expected. I mean it's a lot to take in. Not only did he find out who his mother was but he discovered she was a murderer all in the same evening." The Judge paused. "I always knew that he would have to know but I thought one day I would tell him and try and explain. I didn't want him to find out like this."

"It wasn't the best way but you know at least it's out in the open. It's done now and Patrick will see that it doesn't make a difference to how anyone else thinks of him. He belongs in Hisbury and where he came from and who his parents were doesn't change that."

"You're right, of course you're right. I just hope Patrick is thinking the same way."

"There's nothing you can do. You did the right thing taking him in and you've done your best bringing him up. He's family. Give him time and he'll see that."

"I hope so." The Judge sipped his coffee thoughtfully.

Chapter 38

Patrick Cooks Lunch and More

Sarah spent the rest of the morning relaxing and trying not to think about the case. There didn't seem to be anything else they could do now and they were no closer to solving anything. Sarah pottered around, cleared out some of her old clothes for charity, which she'd been meaning to do for ages and then lay on her bad and finished reading her book. She got so involved in the story that it was only when she finished it and put it down that she realised the time. She quickly changed into a flowery summer dress, grabbed a thin cardigan in case in got chilly and headed off to Patrick's. She had been this way so many times before that she could just let her mind wonder as she walked and invariably her thoughts fell on the case again. There really did not seem to be any other leads to follow. Then smiling to herself she thought she must ask Patrick about what Cookie had said but that would probably just make him laugh. It was nothing to do with the case. Strange though. Having said that Patrick was just a nice person and he treated everyone nicely. I suppose Marie just got the wrong idea.

By now Sarah had reached Patrick's house and rang the bell. Five minutes passed and Sarah felt puzzled and then suddenly Patrick opened the door. He was wearing an apron which was splattered with flour.

"Oh hello," said Sarah. "What are you up to?"

"I am cooking you lunch," said Patrick with a flourish.

"Wow. Well I'm glad I had a big breakfast!" Sarah laughed.

"Oh come on, it will be fun," said Patrick and led Sarah through to the kitchen. "Martha has got a day off and Uncle is out. I was going to take you out but then I thought it would be nice to have the house to ourselves."

"So what's on the menu?" asked Sarah sitting down at the kitchen table and throwing her cardigan over the back of the chair.

"We are having beef casserole and then chocolate mousse for dessert. Is that okay?" Patrick suddenly looked a bit worried.

"That's perfect," said Sarah, her heart going out to him. "It's a lovely idea Patrick. Thank you."

"Well it was so nice the other day when we went to lunch in London, I thought we should do it again. Not that I'm saying the food will be quite up to that standard!"

Sarah laughed. "I'm sure it will be lovely!"

Patrick poured her some wine and they sipped their drinks as the smell of the casserole stole round the kitchen. Sarah felt so at home here.

She turned to Patrick. "Do you remember when we were children? We were always coming in here and scrounging snacks from Martha and taking them out to our den at the bottom of the garden." Sarah smiled. She remembered it as if it was yesterday.

"Oh my goodness that's a long time ago," said Patrick. "And what about that old shed which the gardener didn't want anymore? He had moved into his posh new larger version elsewhere in the garden and he wanted to get rid of the old one but I begged and pleaded with my Uncle to let us have it."

"Yes and we painted it a bright yellow colour as that was the only paint we could find that no one seemed to want and then we furnished it very importantly with a table and two chairs and started a secret society with a password. No one was allowed in without the password or, as I seem to remember, unless they were bringing refreshments."

"Yes the secret clubhouse. And do you remember the name of the club?"

"The TT club. How could I forget," said Patrick.

Sarah laughed and then looked serious.

"Are you alright?" said Patrick.

"Oh sorry, Patrick it's just that I feel so at home here and thinking about all the things we did as children, it seems such a long time ago. With everything that's happened lately, it seems like a different world."

Patrick was about to say something when they suddenly realised the cooking smell had changed for the worse.

"The casserole!" Patrick jumped up, opened the oven and took out the casserole. "Just caught it in time. Goodness I couldn't do this all the time," he laughed.

"Right! Shall we go into the dining room?" said Patrick.

"Why don't we eat in here? It's so cosy."

"All right, you get some cutlery. Should be in that drawer over there," Patrick pointed towards a drawer in the dresser. They laid the table and Sarah sat down while Patrick ladled big portions of the casserole into two bowls and cut some fresh bread into a basket.

"Right! Dig in. I hope it's okay."

Sarah took a little on her spoon and blew it and then tasted it. "Umm. This is delicious. I didn't know you could cook like this, Patrick."

"Well actually I suppose I can't have any secrets from a club member. Martha actually prepared it and I warmed it up."

Sarah laughed. "Well you did an excellent job," she said.

"Thank you." said Patrick. "I have my moments!"

They finished their casserole and then Patrick cleared the plates. "How do you feel about dessert? I did actually make these myself!" Patrick brought out two wonderful chocolate mousses. They chatted as they ate their dessert and an hour and a half later Sarah found herself relaxing in the sitting room with a cup of coffee in front of her, a box of chocolates open on the table and Patrick, after putting on some classical music, sat opposite her and smiled.

"This is so nice," said Sarah. "With everything that's been happening lately, this was just what I needed. A little quiet time, just relaxing. I feel so comfortable with you Patrick. I always have. I suppose us growing up together helps. We don't have any secrets from each other and we can say anything to each other. Speaking of that I've been meaning to ask you about something strange that Cookie said to me. You'll probably find it really funny but I've forgotten to ask you until now."

"What's that?" asked Patrick.

"It was after I found Marie and I was talking to Cookie and she said how sad it was and that Marie was a good worker, a good girl and then she mentioned that she'd got some fancy in her head about you."

"What?" Patrick looked surprised.

"I know. I thought it was strange too. Anyway she said that Marie had got it into her head that you were sweet on her and that you kept complementing her and being really nice to her. Anyway Cookie said Marie must have been imagining it but I've been meaning to ask you about it. I thought you would find it funny."

Patrick looked thoughtful for a moment, as if trying to decide something. In his head he could hear himself saying, "Don't tell her," "She'll never understand." Then somewhere from deep inside him another voice was saying, "It's Sarah. You've known her since you were children. This is what you have both always wanted, to be together." Then he heard Sarah's voice, a little alarmed now.

"Patrick are you okay? You look worried?"

Patrick looked at Sarah and made a decision. "Yes, I'm okay but there's something I have to tell you. Like you said we shouldn't have any secrets."

"Of course you can tell me anything. Is everything all right?"

"It will be once I've told you. Then we can be together. You know we're meant to be together, don't you Sarah?"

"I know how you feel Patrick and I care about you very much but what has that got to do with what Cookie said?"

"What would you say if I told you what Cookie said was true?"

"I would say what I told Brian that you're a nice person, nice to everyone and that Marie just misunderstood. It happens. You never would have led her on."

"I would do anything to be with you and however much you cared for me you never could have married me when I had no money and couldn't provide for you. Now we can get married, we can be together."

"You mean because of Eddie. But Patrick if I wanted to be with you, I would be with you whether you had money or not."

"You think you would but can you imagine years of struggling? Someone else might have looked more attractive to you. I couldn't take that risk."

"You don't mean?" Sarah had gone quite white now and her voice shook.

"I did it for us. Don't you see? I knew Eddie had left everything to you."

"And Jeremy?" Sarah's voice shook but she had to know.

"I didn't plan it but he saw me and Marie together and he probably didn't think anything of it at the time but it would have come out after Eddie was killed and I couldn't risk that. I met Jeremy in the grounds of the Hall and we came in for a drink. Jeremy wanted to see Eddie but I'd seen him head off to towards the village to run some errands. It was easy to put the poison in Jeremy's drink and then I asked Marie to clear up the whiskey glasses and destroy the evidence. I hid Jeremy's body in the hallway cupboard and then, when we were all on the terrace having drinks, I told Marie to drag the body the few feet from the cupboard into the middle of the hallway. She protested and wanted to back out but I told her it was too late, that she was involved and we had to go through with it. By then she was scared and she was sweet on me. It wasn't hard to persuade her. Once Jeremy was positioned in the hall all Marie had to do was scream and drop her tray and we would all come running out."

"And Marie? What would have happened to Marie?" Sarah could hardly get the words out. She stared at Patrick.

"Yes, she was becoming too clingy. I ended things with her after Eddie was dead and I told her no one would ever believe her story but she went to see Inspector Harbury with some story just to scare me and I didn't know what she might say next time. I couldn't have risked it. I arranged to meet Marie in the living room at the Hall but when I got there she was dead. I was shocked. I didn't know who could have done it but I went back out into the garden and then I saw you go in and I followed you and the rest you know."

"So you watched me go in and make that horrible discovery and then you just came in and pretended to be shocked and look after me."

Patrick was silent.

"And it was you who planted my broach by Jeremy's body and the earring in his flat."

"Yes but I did it to protect you." Patrick sounded a bit less sure of himself now. "I thought if the police found evidence against you then they would take you in for questioning. I couldn't have you suspected when Eddie was killed."

"And you went to the police about Mummy and Jeremy to throw them off the scent and told Brian and I that Teddy was so jealous to make us suspect him?"

Patrick's confidence returned. "Well that was just lucky for me really. There was so much else going on in Hisbury that it did help to confuse things. And who would suspect nice old Patrick?"

"So, it was you all along? Wait though, who was it that broke into Jeremy's flat?"

Patrick laughed. "That was Marie. She followed me when I went up to London. She was becoming a nuisance but I have to admit I was glad she was there on that day. She saw Constable Braddon take me away and then she broke the window and ransacked the place to throw them off the scent. It was quite a good idea for her. I was quite impressed."

Sarah had unconsciously stood up and found herself backing away from Patrick until she felt the wooden cabinet that housed his Uncle's collection of china hunting figurines. Her hands behind her back she held onto the wood to steady herself. Patrick came towards her, his voice softer now.

"I know it's a lot for you to take in but I know you will see things my way in time. Eddie wanted you to be happy. You deserve to be happy and I can make you happy."

Sarah suddenly recovered herself and stood up straight. "Eddie loved us both and if you knew me at all you would know that money wasn't important to me and that nothing would stop me being with someone if I wanted to. I had always thought that we would be together but I was thinking of the boy I grew up with not the man you have become."

Patrick stopped in his tracks as if he had been shot. He sank down on to the sofa and covered his face and then suddenly everything seemed to happen at once. Inspector Harbury rushed in from the garden doors straight to Sarah while behind him came two Constables who went straight to Patrick and led him out but everything was a blur to Sarah until Brian came in and then all she could think of was getting to him.

She felt Brian's arms around her and let herself be led back to the sofa and found herself sitting next to Brian. He had moved away slightly, to give her some space she supposed, and then she realised that the Inspector was talking to her.

"I know it's been a shock and I won't keep you long but if you could just tell me in your own words what happened."

Brian handed her a glass and she drank. The brandy restored her a little and she felt stronger.

"Well, there isn't much to tell. I mean you heard most of what happened. Patrick asked me to lunch. We had casserole and chocolate mousse and we were having coffee. I had been meaning to ask him about something

Cookie said to me about Marie getting an idea into her head that Patrick was always very attentive towards her. I thought he would just laugh but he didn't and then he asked me how I would feel if it was true and well you heard the rest. He said he did it for me…" Sarah's voice broke and she heard Brian asking the Inspector if he could take her home and then somehow she was led out of the house, across the lawn.

Chapter 39

Inspector Harbury Asks Why

The Inspector sat in Interview Room One at the police station and opposite him sat Patrick Foley. It was strange, he thought to himself, how someone you have known for years can suddenly seem completely different. All the features of Patrick's face, which up till this evening had always struck the Inspector as, perhaps not overly bright, but kindly, suddenly seemed cruel and calculating but most of all weak. The Inspector realised that Patrick didn't have the courage to accept his life as it was and to offer Sarah the chance to be with a good, hardworking man, even if he didn't have money. The sad thing was that Inspector Harbury knew that Sarah would not have hesitated for a minute to marry a man without money if she thought he was the right person for her. As it was she had had a lucky escape.

"What are you thinking, Inspector? I suppose the usual, why did I do it?"

"I'll ask the questions thank you Mr Foley." The Inspector paused. "Why did you do it?" Even after hearing Patrick's conversation with Sarah he still found it hard to believe what Patrick had done.

"What choice did I have, Inspector? No-one really ever cared for me. My Father left me and I never heard from him again. He died in some far off place without even meeting me and probably not even giving me another thought and my Mother gave me up. Uncle did his duty but he would never have chosen to have a child living with him. All he cares about is his work, even when he retired he carried on consulting on cases and nothing really changed. Sarah was the only person who ever cared for me and I couldn't risk losing her. She said she wouldn't have cared whether I had money or not but that's just something people say. Money is everything, Inspector. It gives you a place in society, it gets you friends and it would have made sure that I kept the woman I love. It was the biggest gamble of my life and I lost. It's as simple as that."

Chapter 40

All Becomes Clear

It was early evening and Sarah felt exhausted. After arriving home, Professor and Mrs Quentin had fussed over her and she was now sitting in the living room with them and Brian when there was a knock on the door and Rose appeared.

"Inspector Harbury is here, Ma'am."

"Thank you, Rose. You can show him in."

"Sorry to disturb you all. I was just on my way home and I wanted to make sure that Miss Quentin was alright."

"I'm fine, thank you, Inspector. I was very shocked but everyone is taking good care of me and I'm glad that you and Brian were there."

"Yes thank goodness you were there, Inspector and Brian," said Mrs Quentin.

Sarah suddenly looked at Brian. "Why were you there?" she asked.

Brian looked embarrassed. "I was worried about you," he said.

Professor Quentin looked at Brian and made a decision. "I think that we all need something to eat and drink," he said. "I will get Rose to bring us some sandwiches and drinks and then Brian and the Inspector can tell us exactly what happened and how they managed to solve the mystery."

Professor Quentin went out and in no time at all Rose brought sandwiches and drinks and laid everything out on the coffee table. The Inspector sat down and for several minutes they all helped themselves and munched away and Sarah felt some of her strength returning as she ate.

"Now Inspector," said Professor Quentin. "Why don't you start at the beginning."

"Actually, I think Brian should tell the story. He really put everything together and came to see me. I think the advantage he had was that he didn't know anyone down here in Hisbury and so he questioned everybody's stories more closely than anyone else did. Even I found it difficult to believe what Brian was telling me when he came to see me. I like to think I would have got there in the end but it's hard to suspect someone that you've known for such a long time and of course the motive was not at all obvious at first, although it was an age old one."

The Inspector looked at Brian and he took up the story. "Well the beginning is really when Mum asked me to come down here and see if there was anything I could do after Eddie's death. I met Sarah on the day I arrived and at first, if I'm honest, I just wanted to spend time with her and the mystery seemed as good reason as any." He turned to Sarah at this point and said. "You have to understand that I hadn't met Eddie since I was a small boy so, although I was shocked by his death, I didn't really know him."

Sarah nodded and waited for Brian to continue.

"Anyway, Sarah, Patrick and I decided to look into the case. Looking back now the Inspector is right I probably was in the best position as I didn't really know anyone involved so I could be more impartial and that's how it started. I decided to check up on everything myself and I actually spoke to Teddy and found he was very different from what Patrick had described. Yes he could be possessive and sullen but he said he knew that Jeremy wasn't the settling down type and so, although he would have preferred it if Amanda wasn't fond of him, he didn't really see him as a threat. This got me thinking and then when Sarah told me what Cookie had said about Patrick flattering Marie, I started to wonder what else was against Patrick. He was found in Jeremy's flat. Could he have planted Sarah's earring? He was first to reach Jeremy's body. Could he have planted the broach? The more I thought along these lines the more I felt at least there were some things that needed explaining. I thought that a lot of these things could be viewed both ways so Patrick could have been using Marie or he could have just been nice and Marie misunderstood. The earring and the broach could have been dropped by Sarah but I wasn't convinced. Just the earring or just the broach perhaps but not both."

"It was just the sort of thing Patrick would have done," said Sarah. "He was never very intelligent when it came to planning. He would always overdo things. He could never leave well alone." She smiled sadly.

Brian looked anxiously at her but continued. "Well the more I thought about it the more I realised that all these clues basically led to Sarah being taken in for questioning and so not being a suspect when Eddie was killed and then I thought who would go to all that trouble to make sure Sarah was safe and again Patrick was indicated. But I knew it would be hard to prove. At this stage I didn't have any concrete evidence unless Patrick confessed and when I heard Sarah was going to lunch I was worried for her. I went to see Inspector Harbury and told him my suspicions. He was sceptical but I convinced him. We took Constable Johnson and another Constable with us to the Hall and hid ourselves and then all we had to do was wait."

"Yes and I must admit at times I thought Patrick must have been mistaken," said Inspector Harbury. "I mean we were waiting all through you eating your lunch and you were chatting perfectly normally and by the time you moved to the living room we were all feeling very uncomfortable and stiff as we'd been still for almost two hours waiting for Patrick to say something incriminating. I was beginning to think it had all been a waste of time until you told him the story about Cookie saying he was flattering Marie and then suddenly it all came pouring out and the rest you know."

"You mean you were there all the time, all through lunch and you heard everything?"

"I'm sorry, Sarah but you wouldn't have listened to me? I wasn't sure myself that I wasn't just jealous of your close relationship with Patrick but there was just too much that could not be explained."

"Well," said Professor Quentin, "Patricia and I are very glad you were there, Brian."

"Yes, we can't thank you enough Brian," said Mrs Quentin. "And you Inspector."

"I was just doing my job, Ma'am and I must admit I was sad to find that Brian was right. Mr Foley has always seemed very pleasant to me and it gave me no pleasure to find out it was him but I am glad that we have found out who was responsible. Perhaps now we can all start getting back to normal."

Sarah had been sitting quietly while her parents and the Inspector were talking until Brian said. "Are you alright?"

"Yes, I mean thank you, Brian and thank you, Inspector. I am glad you were there. I was just wondering why Patrick told me everything. I mean if he hadn't then no-one would have known and he probably would have got away with it."

"Well, Miss Quentin that was his weakness," said Inspector Harbury. "He really did love you and he thought you felt the same way and that you would do anything to be with him so he thought you would understand what he had done."

"I still can't believe it. It feels like it was all my fault," Sarah's voice waivered.

"Try not to look at it like that, Miss Quentin. You haven't done anything wrong. Unfortunately some people are just made like that. For whatever reason the thought of not having what he wanted was too much for Patrick and that caused him to do what he did. You mustn't blame yourself." The Inspector paused, drank the last bit of his coffee and then got up. "Thank you, Mrs Quentin, Professor. I must be going now. I'll see myself out."

"Thank you again, Inspector," said Mrs Quentin. "We're very grateful to you. Goodnight."

"Goodnight." Inspector Harbury left.

They all sat quietly for a few minutes drinking their coffee until Mrs Quentin said. "I hope you will stay on for a little while longer, Brian. It would be nice to spend some time together without these awful murders hanging over us."

"I would love to Mrs Quentin but I think that depends on what Sarah has to say. I would not want to stay unless she is happy for me to be here and by the way I must say that Sarah was dealing with things quite well before I came on the scene."

Brian smiled at Sarah. She found herself smiling back and the atmosphere lightened. "Thank you, Brian. I do really appreciate what you did."

"Well I never would have done it without what you told me about Cookie. Perhaps we should become partners in crime, solving mysteries."

"Perhaps," said Sarah, "although first I think I would like to be part of the other partnership you have been talking about."

"You mean it? Really?"

"I do," said Sarah. She moved across to sit next to Brian on the sofa and took his hand.

"Oh my dears," Mrs Quentin descended on Brian and Sarah and gave them both a hug. "How lovely. You must use the house for the reception and you can live at the Hall. It will be so nice to have you both close and such a nice ending after everything that's happened."

"Well we'll leave you to finalise the plans," said Brian with a twinkle in his eye, as he led Sarah out into the garden.

Mrs Quentin watched them walk across the lawn and turned to her husband. "Such a lovely young man, Charles. I do think Sarah will be so much happier with Brian than with Patrick. I always thought there was something not quite right about that boy."

Professor Quentin smiled to himself and picked up his book.

The End

Printed in Great Britain
by Amazon